Wyld Wynd
The Rising

Peter Sandor

Wyld Wynd The Rising, 2nd Edition.

05-08-25, Rev 19

ISBN 978-0-9917954-5-1

Read other books by Peter Sandor

Contents

Chapter 1	1
Chapter 2	10
Chapter 3	22
Chapter 4	32
Chapter 5	37
Chapter 6	51
Chapter 7	56
Chapter 8	64
Chapter 9	73
Chapter 10	82
Chapter 11	87
Chapter 12	99
Chapter 13	103
Chapter 14	117
Chapter 15	124
Chapter 16	135
Chapter 17	141

Chapter 1

You could see it in his eyes. The fear departed his gray-blue eyes and darkened with a depth of determination. The cold of the gnarled maple tree against his back added to his growing security. After all, this was his forest. He knew it well, and even as random tendrils of moonlight sifted down through the distorted, moss-covered branches, giving the grove of ancient maples an eerie ambience, he felt safety. With renewed courage and a subtle motion, he turned. His face slid against the rough-grained bark until his eyes looked back into the meadow he had crossed in a run, just moments before.

Even though Nolan Harrison's face was half-hidden by the wide trunk of the tree, one could not mistake his boyish good looks, giving him an appearance younger than his 28 years. The high cheekbones and full eyebrows usually brought people's attention to his eyes, now sparkling with reflected light, as a lone, wandering, night-cloud passed from under the half-moon.

Nolan caught the faint movement across the brush-covered meadow. The first of the three intruders who stalked him stepped into a bramble of ferns. With just his face visible above the wide leaves, he panned slowly from left to right across the thicket of maples Nolan was nestled in. He spun back behind the tree with a sudden realization. Just as he could see the moonlit face of the intruder, they would be able to see his fair-colored skin if he was not careful. Silently, he slid further into the shadows.

Ever since he was a boy, Nolan had been enthralled by the forest and nature in general. Fittingly, destined circumstances brought him to the Olympic Forest in Washington State where he had been stationed for the past 18 months.

Momentarily, his memory shot back to his previous life in the city and how a failed marriage brought him to this remote, serene location. It reminded him how life has its twists and turns, and even the worst of situations very often ends, as destined, with a bright ending. However, in this case, this ending wasn't so happy.

A gust of cool wind brought Nolan's thoughts back to the present. His hand reached down to the forest floor, pushing aside the fungus growing at the base of the tree. Digging his fingers into the cool, moisture-laden soil, he pulled a handful up and coated his face with a thin layer of the dark mud. His light-brown hair, cropped short at the sides, fell past his collar at the back, completing his stealthy appearance.

He turned and slid his face around the tree to look at those who hunted him. His face and dark-green denim shirt, merged with the bark. He was now as one with his forest. His lanky, six-foot frame camouflaged into the branches, and his movements blended with the moss as it swayed with a regal splendor, enticed to and fro by the wind that came from the sea coast—some thirty miles to the west.

Barely opening his mouth, he muttered, "Everything happens for a reason. Shit. So why are these three men after me?"

His knuckles turned white, as he pressed them into the tree. He needed the stab of pain to keep his mind focused on the three strangers who arrived earlier in the evening—the three men who killed his partner, John. His knuckles pushed even harder. There was no time, so the grieving would have to come later. Right now, his mind needed to stay focused, or he would be joining John under the shadow of death.

His mind recounted what he knew of the three intruders who stormed into his forest station house just hours ago as the early evening sun was setting. The rugged clothes they wore appeared normal enough for the remote terrain of the mountains. They all wore similar hiking boots, long, dark pants and cotton shirts. Each wore a different non-descript color that would keep them from getting too much notice. They also wore thin leather jackets, although the leather, having a wider grain to it, didn't appear to be a type he'd seen before. That, along with a slight accent to their words which was hard to place, gave Nolan a feeling this wasn't where these people belonged.

All three men were shorter in stature. One had long hair heavily thinning across the top of his head. The other's hair was lighter colored with a distinct military cut. The third man, who seemed to be the leader, had black, gangly, unkempt hair.

The leader was still kneeling behind the tall ferns, considering the meadow that was some 50 yards across. Methodically, his eyes panned from under the crop of black hair across the moonlit meadow as he took in every section of the fern and brush-covered ground. His head stopped moving side to side, as he noticed the plants beaten down in a thin path from his position to the trees ringing the far side of the meadow. Moving his left arm, pointing once to the left, then once to the right, he gave silent directions.

Squinting into the dark background, Nolan saw two dark figures rise and with careful steps move in the two directions the leader indicated. Their footfalls left light crackles as they tread first through the low scrub and then disappeared into the trees ringing the meadow. Nolan knew it would take some time for either of the two men to flank him. Having always been a good observer, his senses told him he would have to be careful. From the hand signals and the flanking movement, he determined the men had military training. Fortunately, he also saw by their hesitation that they were not comfortable in the forest—his forest. He was confident he had the advantage. The three intruders were coming into his world where he had the experience. They didn't know it yet, but these hunters had just become the hunted.

As stealthy as the wolves who sometimes roam the woods, Nolan slipped off to his left with silent footfalls. There was no path here, but he'd learned to use the *forest walk*, feeling as much as walking with his feet. When his foot sensed the pressure of a twig or a dry leaf, it would slide until it felt firm ground. Although it sounded awkward, he was practiced, and his movements were fluid. He could steal through the tangle of thick trunks and bent, low-hung branches with surprising speed and stealth.

His eyes turned up again, catching the moonlight as he reviewed the band of trees just ahead of him. The branches intertwined impassibly except for two arched openings just large enough for a man to squeeze through. Nolan wasn't sure, but he thought the man who had been directed to come in this direction was the heavier set fellow. When Nolan saw movement across the meadow, moving toward his present location, he surveyed the outline of the figure and recognized the crewcut hair and stocky build.

Nolan had a good mind. Not great—but good. He was never considered brilliant, but people remembered him for his good sense for logic. It was what Nolan always described as just plain back-country, common sense. This went hand in hand with the fact he was a great observer. Not a good observer—but a great observer, and in many situations in the past it gave him an advantage.

During the short time John, Nolan and the three intruders spent together at the station house, Nolan took in as much visual information as he could regarding the three. He recalled the stocky man perspired heavily, and didn't appear fit for feats of labor. He would certainly take the shortest and easiest path, Nolan surmised as he crept toward the archway to his right. He only had a few more minutes, and in that time, he needed to find the forest tools he would require.

Once Nolan arrived at the bracken of trees, he reached down into the undergrowth and found four medium-sized rocks he settled deep into his left pocket. He also knew there were usually some thick, fallen branches at the base of these hundred-year-old trees. His fingers circled one having the right girth, and as he lifted, he judged the weight to be adequate. Pulling the limb from the moist ferns, he saw it was also the perfect length.

Nolan silently climbed the gnarled branches, showing his stealth and ease in the trees matched his expertise on the ground. He had been listening and heard the crush of twigs and leaves as the stocky figure's footfalls came closer. Settling in a prone position along a wide branch overtop of the archway, Nolan kept his arms free to hold the thick club-like branch. As he shifted to his right, both shoulders hung off the back side of the thick limb. He took a quick look from his vaulted vantage point back across the meadow to see the leader, still preoccupied with the meadow, warily following Nolan's still fresh tracks across it.

Nolan waited. He slowed his breathing—in through his mouth—out through his nose. *Relax*, he thought. It was a moment where time was irrelevant. The tension of not seeing his foe, yet having the noises of the forest night play over his ears, made moments feel like hours. He fought to keep focused. The attacker would show up soon enough.

The only thing moving was Nolan's eyelids, blinking every 20 seconds. All else was perfectly still except the small insects of the forest, welcoming him to their tree. He felt them crawling on his skin under the loose pant legs and sleeves. Keeping his composure, he didn't let the multi-legged creatures distract him. The danger was not there. Rather, it was coming through the thicket of trees—two hundred pounds of killer now visible, 15 yards north of his perched position.

It was quiet except for the sound of Nolan's heart pressed against the supporting branch. The sound of his heartbeat became even louder, thumping in his ear as the approaching man's movement stopped. In the man's face, he saw the killer was unsure of himself. The darkness and unfamiliarity with his forest was playing on the man's mind as he hesitated and second guessed his path to the location of his quarry. The stoppage was only momentary. He continued onward after inspecting the woods as best he could in the low level of light. The crackle from the attacker's boot as it crushed into the underbrush now drowned out Nolan's heart. The hair on the back of his neck stood on end, as the sounds came toward the opening he hovered over.

The man was nervous. He looked from side to side, and once, he briefly looked directly up at Nolan patterned into the tree. However, the attacker's thinking was two dimensional, and he continued toward the opening. He paused for a moment before turning sideways and shimmying through the tight space. It was an awkward position and became even more so, as he ducked his head down to clear the overhead gnarl of branches.

At that instant, all the killer heard was the club of wood cutting through the air, and the whistle filling the void behind it as it sliced toward the back of his head. That whistle was the last thing the man ever heard. He didn't hear the deep *thunk* as the club made contact with his skull, splitting it open.

Nolan cringed as he *did* hear the sickening *thunk*. It was the first man Nolan ever killed. There wasn't much time to think on it, as these men wanted him, and they had already showed their ruthless intent when they killed John. In his mind, he justified this was about his survival. His natural instincts kicked in, but it didn't stop the *thunk* from echoing in his mind, nor the taste of nausea from overcoming him. The dead fellow's comrades also heard the *thunk,* and the sound of the pair crashing through the brush toward his position cleared Nolan's mind and body instantly. He had to move quickly.

Deftly, Nolan twisted his body off the branch. The free fall landed him on the ground as his bent knees took the energy of the drop. The motion was fluid, and the energy transferred to his muscles as he sprung deeper into the thicket to his right. Almost immediately, he flung the club to his left. Hearing the remaining two intruders still a minute or two away, he squatted in the ferns on a low rise of ground shadowed between two tall trees.

Reaching into his pocket, Nolan pulled the first stone out, flinging it a short distance from where the killing club had crashed against a rock. He listened. The two remaining killers stopped for an instant as they tried to discover the direction of the sound and regain their bearings. Just as quickly, the sound of their fast-paced march through the undergrowth was re-established, with the direction veering toward the diversionary noise. Each of the three other stones was also flung with each landing a little further along a line away from Nolan's location. Between each throw, he waited a few seconds as each rock turned the two intruders away from his location, plowing them deeper into the dark forest.

After the last rock was thrown, Nolan slid down prone with his stomach against the cold ground. Invisible in the waist high ferns, he looked through the stems and listened. His lips turned to a grim snarl realizing the coldness of these men. He didn't know who they were or why they were here chasing him, but he was learning of their character. They had both followed after the path of stones, thinking Nolan fled in that direction. Neither bothered to see if their fallen comrade was dead or alive. Life was expendable to these people—not only John's but also the life of one of their own. The thought of their cold hearts, combined with the chilled night air, sent a shiver through Nolan.

Bringing himself up into a crouch, Nolan moved through the brush and trees on a path parallel to that followed by the two men. Although the men appeared thorough, they weren't creative. He expected they would soon see he wasn't along the false path they were led along. They would double back, in all likelihood along the same path they were now traversing.

With his ears tuned to the sounds of the forest, Nolan was confident the pair hadn't yet backtracked. He used all his forest senses to locate himself in the darkness and to find the winding, shallow brook curving through this part of the forest. Keeping his eyes open and ears alert, he followed the stream of trickling water to where it intersected the beaten ferns trodden by the two men who passed just minutes before.

Nolan gazed left and right, searching out the edge of the brook. He grinned as he found what he sought. Here, the water curved around three large boulders, and a lone spruce was entrenched in the soil directly on the far side of them. The tree was old, surviving in this most often peaceful forest at least ten times as long as Nolan had years on this Earth. Over time, the root structure, in its thirst for water, had twisted and curled around and over the rocks, making a natural, shadowy alcove big enough for a man to hide under. He pressed his frame underneath, between the rocks and the roots. The sparse carpet of long, overhanging grass made him invisible. Pulling the hunting knife from his boot, he forced his breathing to relax as, again, he waited.

Looking from his concealed location, Nolan saw the first set of hiking boots pass by him only three yards away. From his vantage point his sight was blocked from the waist up, but he surmised it was the black-haired leader. He readied himself, flipping the knife in his right hand, so the razor-sharp edge was positioned forward and outward. He counted the seconds under his breath. Surely the remaining fellow with the thinning hair would come in a second, trailing close behind in a covering pattern. Nolan knew he needed to strike and then disappear in the dark before the leader could react. There was no more time to think. A second set of boots appeared, stepping gingerly into the edge of the brook as small droplets of water splashed upward.

It was time to be quick. Nolan hurled himself out from his concealment, bursting toward the figure. With two powerful strides, and without missing the third, Nolan's arm slashed upward. The knife blade sliced through the surprised man's jugular before his head even turned—even before the displaced water droplets splashed back into the trickling brook.

Now was the time for quickness to shift to all out speed, and Nolan accelerated down the far side of the brook. The plan was executed superbly until his right boot just failed to clear the branch lying across the cool water. His body went airborne as he hurtled out of control just prior to the groan of pain, as his body careened across the river stone. Quickly turning, he tried to bring himself to his feet, but his left leg was numb and unresponsive. Looking up, he saw the leader coolly trotting toward him with a confident look filling his eyes.

Nolan's jaw dropped, as he saw the final killer's left hand surrounded by an orange ball of energy. *It must be some type of electrical weapon*, Nolan thought as the glow grew brighter. The man's hand drew back, and in the brightness, Nolan could see pure anger in his drawn face. Whatever his original intentions were, the leader now had only one purpose, and that was to kill him. The fiery hand flew forward, and the energy burst sprung off his fingers.

It has been said in such a moment when you know you're going to die, your life will flash before your eyes. This didn't happen. What coursed through Nolan's mind was disappointment. He had to believe there was a reason John died and a reason he was about to follow. It appeared he would die with that question in his mind, and for some reason, he sensed there were many more unanswered questions. He wondered if his soul would be restless.

These thoughts blurred through his mind in the instant it took for the bright orange burst to come toward him. The hypnotic pattern of thoughts was shattered by the surreal shadow arrogantly bounding from the cover of Nolan's forest. The nimble figure darted between Nolan and the burst. Just before it hit the mysterious figure, a dark-green, luminous haze surrounded the shadowy form. The air crackled with the impact. The shadow swayed momentarily as light spattered across the brook. The clash of energy sources lit the brook with a crescendo of orange and green.

In the light, Nolan saw the last intruder's eyes. He saw the recognition, but it turned immediately to surprise, and less than a moment later, it turned to shock. The man's hand clenched the hilt of the long knife blade embedded in his chest. A subtle movement by the shadow, just a moment before, had the blade accelerating toward the last of the killers. He was dead before his body fell back into the cold brook.

Ironically, the forest was quiet again. Nolan realized his jaw was slack, his mouth hanging open. He didn't know what else this night could bring him as he blinked his eyes in disbelief. The shadow said nothing to him as he walked to the dead man and retrieved his knife. He then washed it in the water, finally wiping it on the leader's coat. The shadow looked over the dead figure, and Nolan heard him whisper out a "hmmm" in what appeared to be recognition.

As the shadow walked back toward Nolan, the moonlight bathed it, and the shadow revealed an unusual man. The first word that came to Nolan's mind as the stranger came closer was *weathered*. Everything he wore seemed so from the worn boots to the faded, dark pants and the even more faded cotton shirt. But the most unusual items were the loose, leather coat hanging slack to his knees and the wide-brimmed, leather hat. Both items gave the stranger a rustic look reminiscent of a time long past.

The stranger remained silent as he squatted on his haunches over the bed of the brook where the burst hit him. Nolan watched as the man pulled open the right side of his worn coat. His calloused fingers reached in, pulling out a small pouch held closed with a draw string.

Nolan, still in shock, began to regain his composure. He noticed there was a deep-red residue on the bank where the two energies came together. The stranger tilted the bag over the residue, whereby a fine dust floated down to cover it. Nolan's eyes opened wide, as almost immediately the redness changed. Some type of chemical reaction blended the residue into the brown background soil, and it disappeared as if the burst had never happened.

Nolan's mind was racing. John was dead. Three other unknown men were also dead. He witnessed bursts of unearthly energy and a silent savior. His temper began to flare, and his eyes narrowed. His voice finally came back to him, "What's this all…"

The stranger's face was still tilted down as he interrupted in a low but direct voice barely heard above the sounds of the forest night. "My name is Daniel. What is your name?"

"Nolan—Nolan Harrison, but hold on. I don't understand any of this. Tell me what…"

The stranger's face flashed upward toward Nolan. Under the curled down brim, Nolan saw the chiseled face almost as weathered as the leather of the hat. Light-blond hair and a thick, blond moustache, gave the man called Daniel a deceptively innocent look. His voice came to Nolan with even more assertion as the sky-blue eyes pierced into him. "*What* you need to know right now is you have five minutes to go back to your station and pack what you can. You need to come with me tonight, and leave everything else behind."

Nolan's face went pale, as the blood drained from it. "Behind…"

Daniel rose, replacing the pouch in an inner pocket and looked down at Nolan who was still sitting in the brook, leaning back on his arms. "Nolan Harrison, your life as you know it is over. You have two choices. Stay here and die—" Daniel's thin lips emphasized the word "—or come with me and live, and the questions running through your mind will be answered."

Not waiting for a reply, Daniel turned, leaving Nolan's gaze somewhere between astonishment and rage. The length of the shadow's leather coat danced along the crisp night air as he decidedly strode back toward the station house. His tall, thin frame became less discernible until it finally disappeared altogether into the darkness of the forest night.

Chapter 2

The Olympic National Forest, covering an area of approximately 1,300 square miles on the northwest tip of Washington State, is one of the most unusual forests left in the United States. In most respects, it has not changed for hundreds of years. The central area is mountainous and is championed by the three peaks of Mount Olympus, reaching 8,000 feet into the air. The majestic mountains, formed from the volcanic activity centuries before, are now permanently tipped with the cold of snow and ice.

Just further down the mountain, tall stands of Douglas fir thrive in the more moderate temperatures, turning the white perspective to a breathtaking sea of blue-green. These thick forests of fir are battered daily by the western sun. Snow melts, giving birth to small rivulets of water snaking down the ever-changing terrain of the mountainside. At these mid-altitudes, barren of man, the black bear, cougar and mountain goat flourish. If there is a god, surely this must be how he envisioned this world.

The constant, moisture-saturated wind from the Pacific Ocean blows across the picturesque landscape from the nearby coast and the ancient forest of 200-foot-high Sitka spruce in the panorama just behind. As the wind passes over the trees, it begins to compress and circle in a turbulent path curled upward by the impending mountains. The clouds struggle in their effort to crown the mountains until, finally, the wind and moisture release in different directions. The cool air cascades over the rugged tips before caressing down the leeward side. Eventually, the heavy condensed vapor falls, adding to the rivulets of water eroding a path down the mountainside. The increased flow of water forms into creeks, and the creeks then feed into streams. Finally, they churn into thick rivers passing along lush shorelines brimming with abundant animal and plant life.

The Quinault River is one such place being so magnificent in its raw beauty. The Douglas firs from the higher reaches give way to Western hemlocks and, in this river valley, to the big-leaf maples creaking in song above the brook Nolan now sat in.

Nolan's mind was awhirl. He rose with a slight wince passing across his face, as the numbness in his left leg was still there, although it had now lessened to a mild sting. He flexed his leg, and there was no permanent damage—just what he surmised was a jammed nerve. His shoulders slumped as he considered his options, including those the stranger, who called himself Daniel, had provided.

Already, Nolan's forest was different. Although the bodies scattered through it were still fresh, the forest stank of death. His chin drooped, and he sighed deeply, realizing this forest would never again have the sweet fragrance of floral life. Death would forever haunt these woods long after the bodies were removed. He could not stay.

Nolan contemplated his course of action as he began the walk back toward the station house. The *United States Department of Forests* would soon wonder why John and he hadn't reported in. They would send others to investigate—three days hence in his estimation, and they would surely find the dead bodies.

Nolan's body froze and he thought, *hell!* They might come to the conclusion I killed John along with the others! His thoughts bounced back and forth. Perhaps his best recourse was to stay and explain what happened. That thought was quashed quickly as a soft, sarcastic chuckle passed his lips. "Shit, I'll explain it. They'll be sure to understand. Three mysterious men appeared, as if out of thin air, and smashed into the station house, grilling John and I for information. They asked ambiguous questions, then took John outside and killed him—and Ohhh," he said as he raised a patronizing finger, "I've no idea what the information they were looking for is." Still talking to himself, he curled his fingers into a fist and hit his chest. "And in that chaotic moment, I was so freaking scared I sped into the woods so fast they had no time to react." His head bobbed from side to side as he continued. "Oh, I did manage to kill two of them when they chased me into the woods, and I was saved from the last one by yet another stranger who also miraculously appeared out of thin air!" Nolan tilted his head, continuing the mocking tone. "And did I fail to mention that they could throw energy bolts from—*their freaking fingers!*" Nolan spit but it didn't clear the taste of bile from his mouth. No one would believe him. He had to leave.

Clearing the meadow, the station house came into view in the moonlight. He saw Daniel sitting on a large, flat rock, his chin resting on his palms with his elbows balanced on his knees. Daniel didn't look up from under the brim of the hat as Nolan approached.

Nolan's words carried the short distance to him. "It seems, at least for the time being, my best option is to take your offer and travel with you."

Not waiting for a reply, Nolan strode deliberately through the doorway and into the storage room at the end of the main hallway. There, hung on pegs on the wall, were two packs fully stocked with emergency gear, a first aid kit and freeze-dried food. They always kept the emergency packs ready to go in case they had to quickly react to an emergency call. He felt the tears welling up in his eyes, as the second pack brought his mind back to John. Having been entrusted with the forest watch, they had spent many wonderful moments gliding over the forest in their Ranger helicopter. It had been a dream job for both of them, but it was time for Nolan to move on. Others would replace them. Within two weeks they would be forgotten as if they had never placed their love and touch on this place. Perhaps it was for the best. In fact, perhaps it was the key. In this haloed place, the unseen touch was apropos.

Nolan's hand pressed out, unhooking his emergency pack, and then he walked briskly to his room. Once there, he slid the pack onto his bed while he pulled open the zipper, then his hands searched through the inner compartments where he pulled out the items he thought were unnecessary. By the time he finished, half the food and medical items were strewn on the bed, considered expendable enough to be left behind.

He walked over to the pine dresser as his eyes focused on the picture of his mother and father in the antique picture frame sitting on top of it. He couldn't help but smile even though his lips quivered. Then the tears finally let go. He promised himself, one day, he would tell them what happened. He gruffly pulled open the second drawer, removed a small waterproof valise and placed the picture in it. Quickly searching through the remaining drawers, he put a few more personal belongings into the valise before re-sealing it. He stuffed this into the back pack along with some extra clothes, and then he was out of his room, not daring to look back, else he change his mind.

Walking back down the hallway, he wiped the memories from his eyes. It was time to move on. Once out the main door, he dropped his pack and said to Daniel, "Help me with John."

"We have no time"

Nolan turned, and his voice rose as his eyes pierced into Daniel, "*He* was my friend. I'm not going to leave him out here for the animals."

Daniel's mouth opened to speak, but he paused, thinking better of it. His eyes relaxed with a hint of compassion. He followed Nolan who already stood over the spot where his friend's scorched body lay. Without words, Nolan and Daniel carried the lifeless form into the station house and laid

John on the long table. Nolan looked down at his dead friend and thought, *please John, forgive me for leaving you here like this.* Nolan crossed John's arms over his chest, hoping the small deed might help his forgiveness. Inwardly, he knew there was selfishness in the act, hoping it would help with his guilt. Perhaps it would be enough of a sign to those who found John, to raise doubt in their minds and to tell them Nolan wasn't a villain. Rather, they should know he was also a victim, not the criminal who conspired the scene they would find when they arrived.

Nolan felt Daniel's fingers fall lightly on his shoulder and heard his compelling voice. "You have done all you can. We must leave now before others come."

"I said I'd come so lead the way. What's the plan?"

Without responding, Daniel paced to the door and out. Nolan following in his steps, pulling the door securely closed behind him for the last time.

Catching up beside Daniel, Nolan angled his head upward toward the taller figure. "You do have a plan, don't you?"

"Hmmm—somewhat of a plan young Nolan Harrison, but remember every plan needs to be somewhat fluid, as I cannot predict all we will encounter," Daniel replied in the most assuring voice he could muster.

Waiting a minute to contemplate this strange man as they walked down the gravel driveway to the dirt path impersonating a road, Nolan snorted. "You don't have a freaking clue what we're going to do, do you?"

Daniel raised an eyebrow as he stared at Nolan with an intentional downward tilt. "I have been watching your activities all day and night. I have been here for some time and have a small camp a little over a mile from here. For your safety, *that* is where we are headed." Daniel made a right turn, having reached the narrow, bumpy road at the end of the drive. "That is the only part of the plan you need to know right now, so don't waste your energy with the chit chat. It's dark, and you need to keep your focus on the road."

Nolan's eyebrows furrowed. He could feel the rush of blood to his face. "Don't you think you owe me some answers? You and your buddies come in to my world, and in a matter of hours, you've turned it upside down. No, in fact, not turned upside down. It's completely destroyed. 'Obliterated' would be an even better word to describe it!"

Daniel rubbed his chin. "Your facts are correct. It has, in fact, been a difficult night for you, and even though you do not know it, you are in shock. At this point, your retention would be quite deficient, and there is much for you to know. I hate to be repetitive, so save your energy."

With his eyes wide and his face flushed, Nolan's words now came in a sputter. "Retention—deficient! Let's get an understanding right now. I said I was coming with you for now, but I'll not be left in the dark. So, let's have some information now, or your walk back to your camp will be a lonesome one. I can do just fine on my own."

"You don't know the character of the people you are dealing with, Nolan. On your own, you would be killed. There are things you need to learn, so unfortunately, even though you do not know me, you must have trust."

"Trust works both ways," Nolan was quick to reply.

The silence of the forest hung over them for a few minutes until it was broken by the calming hoot of a spotted owl perched somewhere high in the canopy. The road was gently angling upward as it weaved through the forest of tall trees. It was a transition of dark shadows and moonlit sections, controlled by the random scattering of hemlock, spruce and maple. On the edge of the road, the oblivious toads and lizards, dining on the multitude of insects, rushed further into the safety of the vegetation, as they sensed Daniel's determined pace.

"Okay Young Nolan, I will answer some questions, but understand there really is much you must learn from me, and in some ways, it is the telling of a story. In this story there is a beginning and an end, but let's not rush to the end. You might not like what you hear, and you will certainly not believe it unless I prepare you."

Rolling his eyes at the disclaimers, but seizing the opportunity, words rushed from Nolan's lips. "Tell me about the energy burst I saw from the hands of those men and your shield which deflected it."

Daniel's footfalls stopped as he reconnoitered his position. The back of his hand casually slapped Nolan's chest as he nodded his chin in the direction of a small grove of Western hemlocks, uphill and to their left. Daniel led the way up in a zigzag pattern, dodging the trees and heavy underbrush as the river valley gave way to the foothills of the mountain range.

"It's not far now." Daniel's words came between heavier breaths. "As for the energy burst—you saw what you saw. It is a weapon unknown to you and many others here in the United States. The same goes for the energy shield you saw around me, deflecting the orange burst."

Nolan's voice carried an edge of irritation. "Of course, I saw what I saw, but where are you from. And this weapon—where did it come from?"

Daniel chuckled. "You move quickly to the end of the story. I have already said here, walking through these woods, you would not believe me. So, I will not answer your question, specifically, at this time." Daniel turned his head, made eye contact, and the soft persuasion again came to Daniel's voice. "Bear with me. My camp is only a moment away. Once there, I will tell the story from the beginning."

Biting his lip, Nolan followed, and as promised, they were at Daniel's camp forthwith. He didn't say it aloud, but he was impressed by Daniel's selection of camp locale. He was standing beside a rock outcrop some thirty feet high. The lower rings of the face were sedimentary in nature while the upper reaches were solid bedrock. Over time, wind and water eroded the lower section so that the upper stone curved outwards, providing natural shelter from the elements. The small shelf hewn by wind and rain was ringed with hemlocks. The tips of the nearest scratched past the rock outcropping and even higher into the night sky.

Nolan always did this. He surveyed a situation or location and absorbed all the information. Seeing the make-shift fire pit ringed with rock and filled with white ash, his gaze stopped for only a moment before looking past it. On the far side of the fire pit was a bed of soft hemlock-needled limbs and a pack, he assumed belonged to Daniel, leaning against the rock wall.

Daniel's finger curled open and pointed to the bed of hemlock. "Rest. It has been a long night."

Nolan followed Daniel's advice, but the adrenalin was still coursing through him. He wasn't ready for sleep, so instead, he sat on the soft bed of needles with his back against the hard rock. He kept his pack close, placing it down beside him.

Daniel was tired. He suppressed a yawn as best he could while he gathered more hemlock branches for a second bed, and dried wood to feed the fire that would keep them warm through what remained of the night. *I'm getting too old for this adventuring,* Daniel thought while feeling every day of his 44 years. He had assumed his days of exploration and *the Watch* were over, but this might well be much too important to leave to others. It was still a long shot, but Nolan Harrison could be one of the *Three Keys* that would release the *Wyld Wynd*.

Wishing to rest his own weary frame, Daniel placed down the bundle of hemlock he would sleep on, and a few minutes later, the dry wood he gathered was alight. The flames reflection danced off the rock face. Lowering himself into a cross-legged position, he reached into his own pack, pulling out two foil-covered energy bars. He tossed one to Nolan, and he tore open the other. A moment later, his teeth were chewing on the contents. The silence was awkward, and Daniel could not hide the unusual look on his face. It was the same look his mother had when she questioned him as a young boy. It was the face of a boy trying to hide some evil deed with an *I don't know* look of innocence.

From across the fire, Nolan finally broke the silence. "Begin the story." He ripped open the covering of his bar. It was not until he started chewing the food that he realized how famished he was, and he quickly devoured the tasty, sweet bar.

The features of Daniel's face flickered in the firelight. "The story begins with the concept of the human mind, or at least, what you perceive it is." He spoke slowly. He knew the words would bring some abstract ideas and difficulty in understanding unless they were laid out very carefully. "The human mind is quite powerful, and as I am sure you know, it is what separates us from animals. The power of our mind makes man the king of this planet, but have you ever considered there might be more to our minds than what you would call 'modern science' knows of it?"

Nolan was trying to show some patience, but he wasn't really comprehending how this related to the chaos of this night as he replied, "No, not really, and not from the scientific aspect you're speaking of."

Daniel tilted his face back slightly, and his features were luminous in the firelight. "But you do read newspapers, do you not? You do watch television and listen to the radio—right? From time to time, I am sure you have heard about psychics, paranormal activities and such—correct?" He watched closely, reading Nolan's reaction.

"Sure. I've seen the odd psychic on a talk show and heard of people who can supposedly read your palm or tell you about your health condition by reading tarot cards," Nolan sarcastically replied. "I still don't see how this relates to three killers in the woods and weapons I've never seen nor even heard of."

Chuckling, Daniel continued. "There are always those who try to act as something they are not, but harlequins and sleight of hand are not what I speak of." He leaned forward. "I am talking about the human mind and very real psychic ability. You might not be aware, but your military has had an ongoing, intensive program investigating and experimenting with psychic ability and the paranormal, for 70 years now. All humans have a low level of psychic ability and some slightly more. These people, who have slightly more, are not readily understood, so your military performs experiments, trying to comprehend and harness their abilities."

"I don't have psychic abilities."

"As I said, all humans do to some extent. Have you not ever had the itch? I am talking of those situations where you are sitting in a restaurant or a library, and for some reason, you think someone is looking at you. When you turn and finally look, sure enough, someone is staring at you."

Nolan's brow furrowed, showing his curiosity.

"Another example," Daniel continued. "Surely you have come across situations where you are with someone while that person says something, and it seems strange since you were thinking the exact same thought at the same time. Sometimes the two of you even say the same words at the same moment. These are latent psychic abilities at a very basic level which *every* human has. But we need to discuss the humans who have a higher psychic level. There are those who have the ability to read thoughts, a variation of that whereby some can project images. Then, there are those who can perform psycho-kinesis which is the ability to move matter. These are only a few of the psychic abilities humankind has."

Shaking his head to clear his growing confusion, Nolan interrupted. "You're trying to tell me these people really exist. I don't believe it. There's an old saying— 'seeing is believing.'"

"That's a narrow view," Daniel was quick to respond. "You recall an inventor named Marconi?"

"Sure. He invented the radio."

Daniel added, "In 1897, to be exact. What do you think his mother thought when he told her he was working on a device where he could send a signal along an invisible wave passing through the air?" He answered his own question. "I am sure she thought it was quite ludicrous, and I can imagine she told all of her family how her son was wasting away his career. Not many from that time period would have believed him."

Daniel saw Nolan shift uneasily as the younger man's analytical sense told him the side note was true enough. Daniel pressed home the point. "Take a deep breath Nolan," he said. "Consider the air you breathe. It is not visible, yet it is an easy deduction that, since it keeps you alive, its reality is as conclusive as its lack of visibility."

"Agreed! But although I can't see air, and I can't see radio waves, I *can* feel the air fill my lungs. I *can* also hear the resulting music from the radio. So, I can see something! I can see the result providing some evidence these things exist."

As his foot slid along the dirt floor of the camp, Daniel kicked a stone toward Nolan. "Throw it at me."

"I want information. I don't want to play games." Nolan really was getting tired as soon it would be morning. His eyelids were becoming heavy, so he didn't want to waste time.

"Throw it," Daniel insisted.

More out of frustration, Nolan picked up the small stone, flinging it toward the older man's chest.

With an electrical crackle, the green haze sprung to life around Daniel's body. Tendrils of darker green shot from point to point in what appeared to be an energy field. The stone hit the field and deflected off, leaving only a small puff of smoke rising from Daniel's chest into the night air. The field was gone as quickly as it came. Daniel paused to hit home the impact of what Nolan saw. "There is some resulting evidence for you young Nolan. That is the second time you have seen it tonight."

Nolan's eyes spread wider, but he wasn't totally convinced. "Okay, point taken, but how does that relate in any way to psychic ability?"

Daniel pulled a small canteen from his pack and threw it over to Nolan. "You must be thirsty." He chose his next words carefully. "Everything has an energy value: me, you, the fire warming us, the trees and the animal life inhabiting them. Each entity has a value of energy. The shield you saw deflecting the rock was created by my mind transferring my internal energy to a different form. Some would call that a psychic event. Energy and how some can, and others would like to, manipulate it, is a critical concept to understand and believe."

It was Nolan's turn to chuckle. "Now that was freaking deep!" He let a few seconds go by while deciding to keep his questions simple. He recalled a saying his father had— "Better to remain quiet and let them think you a fool, than to open your mouth and remove all doubt."

"So why can't I shoot balls of fire?" Nolan lifted the canteen and took a deep draught of water, letting it fill his cheeks before swallowing.

He needed to go slowly Daniel reminded himself. "It is like most—no— all things in life. When a person wants to do something, he needs three things: ability training and desire."

Nolan considered the words before responding. "If I have a desire to use the psychic abilities you say I have, I just need to be trained?"

Daniel threw another piece of dry wood onto the fire, rousing the embers back into flame. They had been talking for some time. "Do you like baseball, Nolan?"

"Sure," Nolan responded as he wondered where this question was going. He adjusted to Daniel quickly, realizing there were reasons for his diversions. He would be patient.

"Let's talk about pitchers. If I recall, throwing a baseball over 95 miles an hour will get you a look toward a major league team, but only a few people have the pure, raw ability to do that. Sometimes it is called—*raw talent*." Turning his hand upside down, he curled his fingers into a tight fist. "However, the raw energy needs to be honed. A person with ability needs to throw the ball at 95 miles an hour, but it needs to be thrown accurately. This comes with training as does perhaps two or three additional miles an hour. So, training is important, but let's not lose sight of the raw ability which must be there to begin with. There are many who want to play in the big leagues, and it will not matter how much training they receive in their lives. Since they don't have the raw ability, they won't be playing anything but neighborhood pick-up-ball. Psychic ability is similar. Some have great amounts of it. For others, feelings of 'déjà-vu' are as far as it will ever go."

"So, we all have psychic abilities, but they are at different levels?" Nolan reconciled his thoughts. It was very hard to believe, and it was confusing him. His face turned downward, and his shoulders dipped.

Daniel's intense words reverberated off the rock enclave they nestled in, abruptly bringing Nolan's shoulders up square with the world. The words were not loud, but they had directness to them and a quiet passion compelling Nolan to listen. "Then there is desire! It is the most important of the three elements. Training will be mediocre at best if there is no desire. For these people who do not have desire and commitment, we no longer talk of their ability. Instead, we talk of their potential. There are many lost souls who had a lot of potential." There was a sneer of disgust on the last few words.

It had been a long night for both of them. Nolan fought the weariness, but a smug grin fought through the fatigue. "You think I have psychic ability—significant abilities otherwise you wouldn't be here."

"Those three back at the station house—" Daniel nonchalantly pointed his finger back through the forest. "—they thought you had ability. I am curious to see if you have ability or just potential. Then again, I might be on, what do you call it—*a wild goose chase*."

Nolan's head was beginning to spin again. New ideas and concepts were muddling his already weary brain, and Daniel wasn't helping. The man talked in riddles.

"Let's talk about the human mind, Nolan."

"Sure," quipped Nolan. He was actually relieved the topic of their discussion was changing.

"What do you know of it—I mean from a scientific perspective?" Daniel questioned.

Nolan decided to use his father's rule again. "Not much really."

Lowering one eyebrow, Daniel continued. "Well, whatever 'not much' quantifies to is even less than you could have imagined."

Nolan shrunk back, duly caught and chastised.

"Here, in the United States, you have the best scientists on this world and the best medical doctors, yet they will be the first to tell you there is much about the human mind they do not know. In fact, what they know the most of is there are areas of the mind they have no clue about—not a clue what function these areas perform."

"I've heard that." Nolan was trying to save some face.

Pausing politely for a second, Daniel continued. "But these areas are not vacant. Residing there is your imagination, your hopes and your dreams— especially your dreams." He saw Nolan's eyes were heavy. "Listen closely now! This is important. Scientists would say your mind is part of your body, and your body is part of this world, and this world is part of this universe that your mind sees." He paused making sure he had Nolan's attention. "It is essential to understand the reverse is actually true. Contemplate it from this perspective. Consider the body is part of the mind as is all we see in this world. Our body is what our mind lets us see. The world around us is what our brain tells us it is. It is a difficult concept to understand, and that is why scientists have never discovered the purpose of these unknown regions of the mind."

Flinging his hands in the air, Nolan looked up and spoke, beseeching the stars in the sky. "Just shoot me now! It would appear we're not really here at all. We're all just a vision from our imagination, locked in a recess of our brains!"

Daniel's voice had an edge to it. "Not quite, but remember what you have heard tonight. All things have energy, and people do have psychic ability." His shield flared to life for a moment before he continued. "And there must be a reason the three killers came after you."

Nolan hated the logic—especially the last comment about the killers.

"I will try again, and I will keep it to the point," Daniel summarized. "There is more to the universe as you would know it. All beings, objects, liquids, gases and anything else that has mass, has an energy value. Collectively, this is the more encompassing universe, or as we call it—the Athar. Remember that word. What your mind lets you see is three dimensional but only on one plane of the Athar. However, the Athar has spatial volume, and there are many planes. In fact—an infinite number of planes exist. One of the things the unknown area of the brain controls is how energy moves from one plane to another in the Athar."

Nolan's hand came up with a finger pointing at Daniel, "You are energy."

"Correct."

"You can move yourself from one plane to another." His finger was still transfixed toward Daniel as the shock of his own conclusion mulled through his mind.

Daniel's soft voice pulled him back. "Yes, young Nolan, as could the three who lie dead in the forest by your station house."

Nolan was now truly drained. The weariness he felt from the physical adventure of the earlier evening, paled in comparison to the mental fatigue he felt from this conversation. His own mind had reached the saturation point, and he needed to sleep.

"Enough," Nolan muttered. He also needed time to think on what had been presented so far. Daniel said the energy shield wasn't a weapon at all. Rather, it was a psychic ability. Daniel had it, and so did the three intruders from earlier this night. Finally, there was this last piece of information stating there were other worlds out there. *Or was it in here*, he thought as his hand subconsciously went up to the side of his head. His mind was heavy with the information, and his head was spinning. He yawned again as he settled himself prone in the bed of soft hemlock branches. Nolan's eyes were having trouble keeping open. He had one last look at the weathered man who sat across from him just as the first rays of early morning sun wove through the hemlocks. Finally, his eyes closed. A new day was coming.

Chapter 3

People generally said Nolan's father was a man of few words, but they also knew when he did have something to say, those few words wouldn't be idle gossip or just an exercise of the vocal cords. He had a way about him exuding respect, and he never lost his cool nor showed his anger, but he didn't have to. When he looked at you, it was always straight in the eye, and there was nothing worse than seeing the look of disappointment in them. Unfortunately, that was exactly what Nolan saw as he sat across the kitchen table from his father this evening.

Mr. Harrison sat in front of his eight-year-old boy whom he loved with all his heart, but a mistake was a mistake, and they needed to be corrected. "Why did you lie?" he quietly asked.

Nolan looked down, avoiding the admonishing look on his father's face. Instead, he focused on his sneaker-clad feet that were crossed and dangling under the vinyl-covered chair. After a few moments, his voice came to him. "I was scared and didn't want to get in trouble."

Mr. Harrison's voice had a high-pitched, soft rasp to it. "Did it work?"

"What work?"

"Did lying keep you out of trouble?" Mr. Harrison repeated.

Nolan's freckle-spotted face tilted up with eyes as big as saucers and welled with tears. "No, Sir!" His tiny voice was shaking as he turned his head vigorously from side to side. "Got me in a heap more trouble!"

"Did anyone get hurt?" Nolan's father questioned.

"Nope."

"Could someone have gotten hurt?"

"Yup." Nolan's eyes were downcast again.

"Your friend Jimmy was lucky. I'm sure you didn't know what asthma was when the day began, but I bet you know what it is now—right?" Mr. Harrison pressed home his point.

Nolan's head bobbed up and down in agreement.

Mr. Harrison leaned forward, placing his hands on the table. "I know it must have seemed funny at the time, when you took Jimmy's inhaler, but when he began to have an attack, you should have said something. Instead, the lie just got bigger and bigger. The hospital is right next to the school, so they got Jimmy there, and he was okay. It would have been a good time to speak up then and face up to what you had done. Even when Lucy said she saw you take it, and the principal questioned you at the school office—still you lied. Finally, you told the truth but only when you saw me."

The look on Nolan's face told it all, and there was genuine remorse at what he had done. "I'm sorry, Dad." The words trembled out.

"I believe you son, and it's good to be sorry. I can also see it's genuine, but you need to learn from these things. I want you to remember one of the rules I live by—*admit your guilt up front*. Think about it, son. We've been sitting here for 20 minutes talking about it. The principal grilled you in the school office for an hour, and that was after your teacher questioned you for the same length of time. If you would have fessed up to it right away, it would have been over in a minute. Sure, you would have gotten in trouble, but what are people going to do? It doesn't make sense to chastise you for hours when you already said you did it."

Nolan's face cracked a small, proud smile. "Dad, last week I snuck a chocolate bar and ate it in bed."

Mr. Harrison burst into laughter. "I think you're getting the hang of the truth thing!" He held his stomach as it jiggled. Then, the laughter faded as did the vision of his father who Nolan missed desperately.

Nolan's dreams had a commonality to them. Perhaps everyone's dreams were like this, bouncing around from place to place and from time to time— like watching a nonsensical home video. This dream was no different, although the evening's adventure was directing the flow. It pulled him in and out of his past, recounting his memories, both good and bad. His subconscious mind drew strength from the good and learned from the bad.

He drew strength from his father who, along with his mother, raised him in small-town Somerset, Pennsylvania. His public school did survive him. He took *truth* to heart, and it added to his creativity, so he didn't give up on pranks altogether. He just learned to plan them better, leaving no permanent damage and only a smile on the faces of those he touched.

The dream was on fast forward as it moved through his adolescent years. Clips of him and his friends flashed past his mind's eye. He was older now, and the vision of his high school was now in the frame—the high school he left during grade eleven.

The dream changed him from the small boy sitting across from his father. Eventually, even in small-town-America, childhood innocence is lost. War, famine and crime in the world, will do this to those willing to listen, and Nolan was a good listener and a great observer. He grew up, developing his own beliefs of what was right and wrong, molded by his ideals of truth and honor. His determined opinions set him apart from others. In some ways, it made him a loner and, in many others, somewhat of a rebel.

Ironically, even though he left school, he intuitively knew the key to life was learning. He had a never-ending search for enlightenment, but not in the spiritual sense, as he wasn't a religious young man—at least in the pure sense of the word.

Consequently, Nolan was driven to read. He read books, newspapers and the internet in his obsession to absorb life, and when he finished reading, he would read some more. He learned more than he would ever have picked up in a regimented, school system.

The vision of him lying back against his headboard, reading, vaporized, and an older version of himself appeared. His hair was cropped short, and he was in a military uniform. He didn't know why he joined the Air Force. There wasn't any pressure, as his parent's supported him in all he did. They truly loved him. Thinking back, Nolan considered, at times, his decisions were directed by his search to find a place to fit in.

For a time, his passion for learning was satisfied since he was assigned to a helicopter maintenance team. He ate it up, attended all the required training while also signing up for almost every other course he could fit into his schedule. His scope expanded as he not only satisfied his appetite for knowledge, but his lifestyle also changed during his four-year stay in the Air Force. He learned to take care of his body, becoming fitter than he had ever been. However, even though the Air Force gave him so much, even here, in time, he maxed out his stay. He needed more, and it frustrated him to no end, not really knowing what the real cause was. He considered that perhaps, deep down, every man wants to leave his mark on life, and he knew, for him, it wouldn't happen here.

The film scrolled forward and refocused, now on his wife standing on the miniscule front lawn of their suburban townhouse. Nolan changed direction, thinking perhaps his role in life was founded in grass-roots and family life. But after four years it was over, and with self-confessed finality, he left the middle-class life with nothing but the guilt of a poor decision.

However, he felt wealthier than ever as the dream now had him flying free as a bird through the intermittent clouds above Olympic National Park. As only the magic of the dream world can provide, the helicopter materialized around him, as did his friend John sitting in the pilot's seat to his left. He looked over to see John's helmeted head turn, revealing the mirror finish on the impenetrable goggles covering his eyes. His lips opened, revealing a pearl-white smile just underneath.

John knew Nolan didn't mind the flying, but if the turbulence was excessive, John would chuckle, seeing Nolan's fingers balled into fists to distract the tension from his mind. It was at these moments when John would use his sick sense of humor.

"Hey Nolan!" John laughed through the microphone attached to the helmet. "You look like you're afraid of flying, but flying is cool! It's the falling I'd be worried about!" The guffaw was loud as he banked the helicopter sharply to his right. The thin side door of the helicopter, as it shifted from a vertical to horizontal position, was the only thing keeping Nolan from a four-thousand-foot drop to the forest below.

John was gone. The helicopter also dematerialized, and Nolan was tumbling in a free fall through the sky, but there was no fear—just the momentary awe of free flight. The ecstasy was replaced by a sharp pain, as he crashed through the upper canopy of branches and leaves.

He felt the stab of pain again, but this time it was centered in his leg. His subconscious mind faded rapidly. He realized the forest sounds and smells were in the real world. The pain was from Daniel's booted toe prodding into his leg.

"Wake up, Nolan." Daniel's voice spilled down to him.

Nolan was in the lucid state between fantasy and reality. Another sharp prod of Daniel's boot tipped the balance, and the comfort zone of his past faded. His eyes finally blinked open to the bright midday sun. The blinding light forced his eyelids tight, and his arm instinctively came up over his face. There was an unusual ache as he moved his arm. "Christ!" He flexed his arm, prying his eyes open to the sight of Daniel hovering over him with a plate in his hand.

Daniel had a wide smile on his lips. "It seems you are a little soft." The smile turned into a chuckle.

Sliding up to a sitting position, Nolan replied, "You're in an awfully good mood this morning."

Daniel squatted down. "It's early afternoon," Daniel corrected while his free hand pointed to the high position of the sun through the curtain of trees. He pressed the plate containing the hot, *quick and ready* oatmeal under Nolan's nose. "Eat."

Nolan's hand reached out for his pack, but it wasn't beside him. It had been moved and was leaning against the rock wall.

"Worry not. I did not want to wake you, but I was hungry, so I prepared some of the freeze-dried material." Daniel's chin nodded toward the plate. "Eat."

Nolan ate in silence as Daniel began to break camp. It was obvious Daniel was much more jovial than the night before. Nolan was curious why, but his hunger focused his mind on the spoon shoveling the oatmeal into his mouth, and, consequently, he made short work of the meal.

"Shortly, we will need to move on, but I need to know a few things from you first, so I have a few questions," Daniel stated.

"Is this in reference to the fluid nature of your plan?" Nolan winked at him.

Daniel could not help but smile back. "Yes, it is." But his tone quickly became more serious. "As much as you need me to keep you alive, I also need you. I am not familiar with this area of the United States, and, in my estimation, it is an area we will need to obscure ourselves in for a week or two. Is there a place nearby where we can obtain supplies?"

"The only local place is the town of Neilton, although calling it a town would be an exaggeration. However, it's the only place we can get supplies, and fortunately, it's only six miles east of this location."

Daniel nodded, "We will leave in a few moments, but I do need a few more pieces of information, if you can recall them."

"Sure."

"Although it might be painful for you to think back, I need you to do so. Think back to the time you spent with the three intruders at the station house. In a general sense I know who they were, but a more specific identity will assist in determining our next course of action," Daniel said as he squatted down on his haunches in front of Nolan. "Do you remember any of them saying anything about where they were from, or what they were looking for?"

The fingers of Nolan's left hand came up, combing through the short hair on the side of his head as he thought back to the previous evening. His analytical mind liked to put things in chronological order, and he did so here. "They burst in the front door about 6:30 in the evening. Grant it, they didn't exactly have to break in. Who would've thought, deep in the forest, we would need to keep our doors locked?" Nolan snickered. "They carried guns, but they looked different from what I've used in the past. It's strange now that I think about it. Why did they have guns if they had the power to throw energy bursts? Just as strange is the fact they never did use the guns."

Daniel filled in the blanks. "I would surmise the three were a typical exploratory unit, and they would not want to show their psychic power unless absolutely necessary. Based on what I know of these types of forays, they probably did not have time to charge their weapons, but you would not have known that. They knew the sight of them would be adequate intimidation." He nonchalantly waved his hand, pushing the topic to the side for the time being. "I will explain more of that later."

Nolan continued his recounting. "Larry kept his gun on us while Moe and Curly searched the station house…"

"Stop—Larry, Moe and Curly?" Daniel looked befuddled.

"C'mon. The Three Stooges—You know—'wa ba ba ba.' They looked like the Three Stooges."

There was a blank stare on Daniel's face.

Nolan gave his head a little shake from side to side, "Forget it."

"What?"

"Hell, everyone knows the Three Stooges," Nolan mumbled. "I might just be beginning to believe you're not from this world."

Nolan came back to Daniel's question. "Once the three strangers secured the station, they began to grill us. The questions were about what we had been doing. Oddly, they were focused on who had been sleeping that morning. Considering the guns pointed at our chests, we told them what we knew."

"And that was?"

"We both slept the night. John had the early shift, and I had slept in late. I don't remember all their questions, but it focused on the morning hours. It wasn't much later when two of them took John outside." Nolan's voice cracked with emotion.

"It's important Nolan. Think hard. Was there anything they said that sounded like a location or a name? Was anything they were wearing unusual that might identify them?" Daniel probed.

Nolan's lips twisted into a crooked line as he pulled back the memories. "No—no names as I remember, and their clothes were pretty ordinary." He searched his mind, and then his face tilted up. "The ring was unusual."

"What ring?"

Nolan replied, "One of them was wearing an unusual ring on his finger. It was a wide band of silver taking up all the space between the hand and the first knuckle, but that wasn't really what made it unusual." He pointed to the little finger on his right hand as he continued. "There was a raised letter *K* on the surface of the ring. The lower leg of the *K* didn't just end. It continued, circling around the finger…"

"…three times." Daniel finished the sentence. With an ominous sigh, he said, "I know who it is we're dealing with, and we are in more peril than I assumed. I have seen the ring before on people from the State City of *Kaezzar*. Unfortunately, they are not a small troop of vagabonds. Rather, they are organized and resourceful. Once they discover the plight of the exploratory team they sent, they will most certainly return in larger numbers."

"I've never heard of Kaezzar, and it seems everything you tell me just adds to my confusion," Nolan admitted.

"Remember—I told you there were other planes of reality in the Athar. Kaezzar is in one of those planes. It is a highly organized city state, and the people who inhabit it are dangerous to us," Daniel replied. "We better move, Young Nolan."

Nolan held any further questions since he knew they would have to move briskly to get to Neilton before nightfall. He accepted what Daniel told him thus far, mulling over the unearthly testimony as he prepared his pack for the day's journey.

They both took a last walk around the camp, making sure nothing was left behind. Daniel slid into his long leather coat, then placed the worn hat on top of his head, again looking like quite the conundrum. Everything was placed in their respective packs, and each of them slung the weight over their shoulders. They left their overnight lair, striking down the hillside with Nolan in the lead. However, this time, instead of taking the road, Nolan pressed into the forest, leading them east toward Neilton.

Both travelers enjoyed the hike. The terrain undulated up and down in varying degrees. Some hillsides were easy to conquer while, for others, they had to aggressively climb to reach the next plateau. Discussion was nonexistent as the alluring elegance of the forest captivated them in a spellbound trance. As they progressed, the amplified beauty of each new hillside and meadow strengthened the spell. The wildlife sang to them as they traversed the canvas of Mother Earth. All the colors of creation's palette could be seen mingled together in a way no mortal artist could ever reproduce.

They stopped only once. The stream crossing their path was cool, and this was an unusually-warm June day. Neither of them had bathed for almost two days, so they took the opportunity, pulling off their shirts, shoes and socks. Their hands dipped into the cool water, ladling it over their exposed skin while rubbing briskly so as to not let the cold of the mountain stream set in. Nolan dunked his head into the chill stream, and Daniel followed suit.

Daniel pointed up to the position of the sun as the rays passed in and out of the towering spruces crowding this part of the forest. "We better move. It is getting late."

They donned their clothes and continued the trek across the forest terrain. The general direction was now downhill, and Nolan knew they were close to Neilton. His curiosity and innate appetite for knowledge pulled him from the forest's subtle trance. "Daniel, I'm still not sure why the three intruders were after me, or even how they found me."

"You had a dream."

"I have many dreams, but I don't understand why they'd want me just because I dream?"

"You have psychic ability, and it would appear, on the surface, you have a significant amount of it. There are others like you who, from time to time, show up across the various planes of the Athar. I am speaking of humans who unknowingly have extensive psychic ability." Daniel stepped over a long-fallen nurse log covered in lichen and fungus. "We have the means to watch the Athar, and that also means there are ways to camouflage and hide what we look for as we watch. It is a cat and mouse game between two castes of humans vying for survival in the Athar. Yesterday, you were the mouse, and the three Kaezzarites were the cat." He chuckled. "At least, that was what they initially intended."

Nolan turned his head back to look at Daniel. "What about you? Are you a cat or a mouse?" He didn't expect a response. Both of them knew the answer, and it was better left unsaid.

Above them, two birds squawked in a mid-air duel that broke the pregnant pause of silence. "Tell me about the dream you had," Daniel asked.

Nolan's words came intermittently as he was careful of his footing in the cramped vegetation. "I've always had vivid dreams, but the one I had the night before last seemed very real. For many dreams I recollect parts of it, but this one I can remember in detail." He took a second as he hopped over a fallen log. "This dream was strange but perhaps not so weird if I consider the company I've been keeping of late!" he said as he laughed. "It was like I was taking a tour of an unknown place—one unlike any place on this world. I was hovering in their sky, moving over what appeared to be cement-walled cities dotting a primarily sand-covered terrain. The people living in the city looked much like us, and the part which really shocked me was what I saw when I looked across the night sky. There was another planet right beside the one I was floating over. Mind you, not a moon. It was huge!" Nolan threw open his arms. "It covered half their sky!" He turned, winking at the older man following him. "I'm one sick puppy, don't you think?"

Daniel put his hand on Nolan's shoulder, bringing himself in line with the younger traveler. "Listen carefully. That place you saw was real. I don't know what plane it is on, but what you saw was *very* real."

"Freaking hell, man! It was just a dream."

"How do you think we found you? I told you there are people who watch the Athar, and what happened to you is not uncommon. Control of psychic ability, and more specifically, transposition, requires the human mind to be in a relaxed state. That is why, quite often, the first indications of ability show up when the person is in a dream state."

"Transposition?"

"Yes, the moving of your being from a world on one plane to a world on another plane."

Nolan stopped and turned to face Daniel. The look in his face told the leather-clad man he wasn't going further until he had a better understanding.

"Your energy—call it your soul, if you like, transposed across the Athar to some unknown place, and you peeked in. If you remember, I told you there is much to be said for training. It will give you technique, so you can move more discreetly from plane to plane." Daniel's finger came up to point Nolan square in the nose as his voice became lower. "That dream of yours opened up a rift in the Athar so wide it disrupted and rippled the energy field for five minutes. I have never seen anyone do that, and I would suggest neither did the Kaezzar watchers who monitor this zone of the Athar. Nolan Harrison, you are a valuable quantity, and they want you." The last words trailed off as Daniel was already a few yards further toward the road leading to Neilton, now visible in the distance.

The sun was quite low in the sky as Nolan walked along a line of hemlock trees for the last few yards toward the small town. Nolan kept his eyes on the strange man just ahead of him who he was enlisted with. The sun's broken rays pulsed through the tree's limbs, alternating the leather-clad shape in and out of the shadows.

Something inside Nolan told him he better keep his distance until he knew more. He thought, *it's been a good science lesson, but there's something else here you haven't told me.* The older man filled in many blanks within Nolan's mind, but there were still two very large unanswered questions. *What's in it for you, my mysterious savior, and why would you give a shit about me? Everyone wants something, and you still haven't told me your freaking agenda.*

Chapter 4

He stood behind the chair occupied by the senior watch attendant as his fingers tapped repetitively on the metal, high-back frame that fit in nicely with the bland appearance of Watch Room Three. The room was painted clinical-beige, and the pot lights in the ceiling were kept dim, so the large video screen covering the far wall was clearly visible.

Julian pulled his fingers back from the chair and moved them to clasp his other hand behind his back while rocking impatiently on his feet—toe to heel. The black high-top shoes were compulsory for those enlisted in *Watch Command* as was the teal suit he wore over a gray, short sleeved shirt. The suit jacket was casual with a zippered front and a short, upright collar framing the low turtleneck of the shirt. Julian's uniform was the same as those worn by the others in the room except for the three short copper bars on his jacket collar, signifying his command rank. He glanced down, satisfied, seeing the crisp pleat in his trousers, and he kept just as sharp a fold in the sleeves of his jacket. Fueled by his ego, it was a small thing, but he needed it as a token separation from those around him.

Julian often found himself inwardly distracted, but he eventually brought his concentration back to the screen. He was very familiar with the view of white and yellow lights on the black background, and each of these highlighted markers was engrained in his own memory of the energy field. Still, it did not stop him from inspecting marker locations just to make sure nothing had changed. As watch commander of Quadrant Four, he did receive regular reports from the Kaezzar Exploratory House with regard to new markers they had placed, but he needed to see for himself. His brows furrowed with disdain, thinking the incompetence of the exploratory staff was, in all likelihood, even greater than the watchers here at Watch Command.

The view on the wall monitor went out of focus for a moment. Suspecting the cause, Julian's eyes were drawn to the picture window on the left side of the room and the smaller room he could see through it. Therein, Edwin Curic lay on the reclined chair in the drug-induced, comatose state required to tap into his brain. A ten-strand cord from the wall monitor was connected to the adapter in the base of Edwin's skull, allowing his mind's eye view of the Athar to be transferred from his cortex to the panoramic screen. The senior watch attendant was already turning a dial to increase the level of melatonin, that was on an IV drip, into Edwin's arm.

"Not so far, or you'll lose the screen altogether," Julian quipped. "This is one of the first things you were taught in basic training, Coreman."

The senior watch attendant turned the knob back slightly, and the visual came crisply back into focus.

"Edwin is rated as a psych level nine, but he seems to be getting weaker. For eight years now, we have used him to scan the Athar, but, more and more, his mental image is harder to keep in focus. I might just cut him back to four-hour shifts." Julian liked to hear himself talk, notwithstanding his irritating, monotone voice. At his level of arrogance, he didn't care if people were listening, or not. He assumed if they didn't, it was their loss. He continued to complain. "Someone should go over to the Psych Evaluation Center and straighten them out. Incompetence—that's what it is."

The senior watch attendant and the co-attendant sitting beside him, glanced at each other. The look did not need words, as the lack of respect was easily read in their eyes.

Mercifully, Julian's lecture was interrupted by a squeak, as the door to the room was opened. He heard the metallic *click* of footsteps coming toward him. The short, thick high heels Sub-Commander Rankin wore irritated him. It wasn't the noise. It was the thought she was trying to be different. Nobody in the Watch was different—except him.

"Sub-Commander Rankin reporting, Sir."

Julian pulled his hand from behind his back and looked down at his watch. "It's five minutes after eight, Sub-Commander. You're late," he chastised.

"I wanted to be…"

Julian cut her off. "Just the report, Sub-Commander. Update me on the massive rift we saw in the field. What did Green Squad find?"

"They haven't reported in yet, Sir."

Julian turned and faced the taller woman. Still thinking of the high heels, his eyes bored into her. "In the 'Kaezzar Watch Code,' how often are squads on planer hops supposed to report in?"

"Every 24 hours, Sir."

"It has been 26 hours." Julian looked at his watch again. "I should have been called earlier."

A bead of sweat appeared on Sub-Commander Rankin's forehead. "I was handling it and was about…"

Julian was not in the mood to hear her prattle and cut her off again. "Next time, if someone reports in late, call me immediately." It wasn't that he didn't trust Rankin. He just didn't believe Rankin could handle things, but then he didn't know of anyone in this organization who he considered to have superior ability. In his opinion, she was a mediocre officer, at best, and that was what he wanted. He didn't want an assistant who would connive and conspire to better him. People he could lead without too many questions were a top priority, and Rankin was perfect for that.

On the other hand, Julian assumed Rankin thought she was quite something. She'd moved up through the rank quickly, and in his mind, it was because she was a female filling a quota. After a month of service in his unit, he concluded she must have a *godfather* somewhere, pushing her up the ladder, and it irked him. He didn't know who that was, but he would find out. He always did.

The hidden surveillance camera he arranged in her apartment hadn't yet yielded a name, but he picked up enough smut to keep her in check when the need came. *Colir* was an illegal, hallucinogenic drug, and she was a user. At least he had some leverage on the woman, and when he needed the push, Rankin would do whatever he told her to—legal or not.

Sub-Commander Rankin wore an open-mouthed, embarrassed look on her face. Julian left it there as he turned back to the wall monitor while addressing the senior watch attendant. "Attendant Kirlew, bring up the tape of the Athar showing the rift we saw yesterday."

"Of course, Sir." His fingers danced over the keyboard. The live feed of the Athar was minimized to a lower corner of the screen—picture-in-picture format. The rest of the screen showed the tape of the previous day, and initially, it looked exactly the same as real time Athar.

Julian knew it was coming and there it was. In the upper left corner of the screen there was a local distortion over marker 23-1127-4. He marveled again at the size of the rift. Judging anomaly strength in the Athar was subjective, but the size on the screen, the haziness of the distortion and the length of time to come back to clarity, was an obvious indication this was an extremely strong manifestation. He couldn't help but see this as an opportunity fortuitously dropped into his lap. He needed to keep this quiet, so once he solved the puzzle, he could take credit for it. He thought to himself, *wonderful!* I might finally be able to work into the promotion I should have received long ago. "Sub-Commander, were there any other anomalies from this point to the transposition of Green Squad to Marker 23-1127-4?"

"No, Sir."

"Did you check all bands and frequencies?"

There was a slight hesitation in the sub-commander's voice, "Yes, of course."

Julian knew keeping mediocre people around him was a double-edged sword. He could control the adequate people he kept in his Watch Room. This was more important than having top people who would go over his head, both with information and accolades. He also knew there was a price to pay in more double and triple checking on his part.

"Attendant Kirlew, zoom in on 23-1127-4—20 times magnification— and what is its district name?"

Sub-Commander Rankin almost exploded with a response as she hoped to make amends. "The inhabitants call it Earth."

Julian placed a finger on the senior watch attendant's shoulder. "Apply a 40 hertz filter—gamma band only, and let's double check on fast forward. I don't have all night."

The video rolled, and they saw the unknown distortion again, followed by a lengthy space of inactivity until they saw the three small distortions of Green Squad's transposition.

Hmmm—*nothing*, Julian thought as he rubbed his neatly trimmed moustache, stroking down to the thin beard. "Let's go through each of the other four brain bands. I want to see beta, alpha, theta and delta."

The attendant complied, and after all four additional filters were tested, Julian's eyes held a hint of anger. *Nothing. Damn! I need this.* "Attendant, switch from panoramic to sinusoidal view, and filter out the nearby markers. I want to see Earth only and each wave length again. Begin with gamma."

The attendant did not need to be creative. He knew the best way to work with Julian was to just do as he was told. He went through the different wavelengths, but now the view on the screen was of a sinusoidal wave rolling evenly up and down as it crossed the screen in a curved motion. The rift showed again as a massive distortion of the waveform, crackling with peaks and valleys. The disturbance settled down to a normal wave until three small spikes showed, again indicating Green Squad's transposition.

Julian had them repeat the process uneventfully until the theta filter was applied. Julian's finger darted toward the screen. "Yes! There it is! Did you see it?"

On this filter, a very small spike was visible between the large disturbance and Green Squad's hop.

Julian's voice had an *I told you so* air of snoot to it. "Well, it would appear someone else also saw the rift and beat us there. They also took the trouble to mask their hop in a very clever fashion. He fooled almost all of us now, didn't he?"

Everyone in the room knew better than to answer.

Julian's ego was sky high, and he made no efforts to hide it as his words came through a smug grin. "If you think you can calculate it, what's the time lapse from the major rift to this smaller disturbance, Attendant?"

The attendant took a few seconds on the keyboard before replying, "Two hours and sixteen minutes."

Julian turned on his heel to face Rankin once again. His voice had a beguiling ring of cold steel. "I don't appreciate having to do everything myself. Get this team in order and quickly. In the meantime, you will bring *all* decisions to me, and *all* reports are for my eyes only. He headed for the door as he issued his final orders to the sub-commander. "Deploy Red Squad—nine-deep, and I want them on Earth in one hour. I also want a communication runner to personally report back to me every six hours. If you can't figure it out, this means I'll be waiting in my office at 4:00 in the morning."

"Get it Right!" were the last words uttered by Julian before he slammed the door shut behind him.

Chapter 5

"Do you know how long it has been since I have had a hamburger?"

Nolan chuckled. Daniel's focus went right back to the burger as his teeth took another calculated bite. It was obvious Daniel didn't want an answer to his rhetorical question. Nolan was halfway through his own burger, and he had to agree with the look on the older man's face. The greasy burger was damn good.

It was 8:30 in the evening when the two travelers arrived in the small town of Neilton. It wasn't a typical resort village with trademark restaurants and two-hundred-dollar a night hotel rooms. This place was an out-of-the-way accident occurring years ago when a small patch of trees caught fire in an unusually dry summer spell. True to form, bad things tend to bring opportunity with it. Jake Neilton, who manned the railway station and owned the land, decided to partition and sell. The rest, as they say, "is history," and available in touristy newspaper format at the Local General Store for $4.99. Jake Neilton was long gone as was the high-pitched whistle of the steam train, but the simple-life aura Jake lived, remained. It was engrained in the hardliners who now called this humble place home.

Daniel and Nolan had walked down the main, paved road. Appropriately, the plain, painted, steel sign they walked under read - *Spruce Street*. There must have been flooding from time to time, as the sidewalk on this side of the road was raised up on two-by-fours covered with wood planking. The gap under the spruce planks caused their footfalls to echo across the small town.

It took them all of ten minutes to reach the other end of the sidewalk that signified the far border of town. Daniel had poked into Nolan with his elbow as his stubbled chin pointed toward the curtain pulled back at the window of one of the clapboard houses fronting the other side of the street. "Do you get the feeling not much is kept secret in this town?"

They crossed the street and walked back in search of a bed for the night. On this side of the road there were six smaller, dirt-covered lanes cutting off the main road, and none of them were longer than a hundred yards.

These lanes were occupied with more clapboard houses and the occasional upscale board and batten home. Even in the twilight, Nolan could see the dark color of many of the houses. *The rustic hardware store on the other side of Spruce Street must have had a recent sale on dark-blue paint*, he thought.

There were darker shadows on this side of the road. The incandescent glow of the three street lights on the opposite side barely let them see where they walked. They looked up each lane, and on the other side of the grouping of quaint houses was a brighter light. Someone paid homage to the past and kept a light on at the old, boarded-up monument. The light illuminated a freshly painted sign that read -

Pacific Western Railway Station Neilton Stop

Closed for the Season

The aged rails were now rusty with lack of use, as the era of rail was over, and Neilton served only as a stopover point for people who came to this forest to challenge it. Some brought their SUV's—some brought their mountain bikes, and others hiked through the wilderness for the enjoyment only the strangest of breeds gained in inflicting pain on their bodies. Only the real hardliners came to this simple, rugged town, and prime season was still a week away. Consequently, the town was meager of activity.

Their search stopped, as they were confronted by a faded wood sign leaning unsteadily on a front lawn infiltrated with weeds. The sign read - *Simmons Bed and Breakfast*. It took some time for the door to be answered. That, along with the look on the old man's face, told Daniel they were the first patrons to come by in some time. Nevertheless, the room was arranged in short order. They dropped off their packs before heading for the restaurant they were now in, discussing the merits of fried foods.

Their hunger had kept the conversation light, with just an occasional look back and forth. Nolan's face turned to a look of curious amusement as he watched Daniel eat. He was thinking back, wondering if he ever saw anyone eat a burger the way Daniel was going about it. He couldn't hold back the question, "Who taught you to eat like that?"

The older man took a second in between chews to respond. "Is there something wrong with the way I am eating?"

Nolan put the rest of his burger down and started on the fries, two at a time. "I suppose there isn't anything wrong with it. It's just I've never seen a burger and fries eaten in such an *artistic* manner." He tried but failed to stop the laugh as he covered his mouth with his hand to keep the fries from falling out.

Daniel straightened up and put down his burger. "Okay, it would appear I have found a way to amuse you. Let me in on the joke. Hopefully, I will find it equally as entertaining and be the nightcap I have been looking for after this wonderful day of relaxation." He crossed his arms in a cynical posture that demanded a response.

"Alright—let me paint the picture for you. Here we are in a third-rate restaurant in this backwoods hick of a town." Nolan pointed at Daniel's plate and was having a difficult time holding back the laughter. "But that plate of yours has humorous irony all over it. I mean—c'mon—I became curious when I saw you playing with your fries. It was like you couldn't handle their disorganization. You probably weren't even aware you've been straightening them out, little by little. HAAA!" Nolan picked up one of his own fries, mimicking the older man. "Eat one—fix two—eat one— rearrange three." The intermittent snickers continued. "But the killer is your burger." Nolan made a circle over it with a downward pointed finger. "Burgers are greasy. I don't care which restaurant or fast-food establishment you get it from. There is a combination of meat, grease and some messy condiments, and normally half of that combined mess is dripping onto the plate, but look at that!" He laughed again. "There are little bites all the way around the burger in a complete circle, and now you're working on a second circle. It's so freaking systematic! The rest of the world just starts at one side and works their way to the other until they find there is nothing left but greasy finger tips covered in mustard and ketchup."

Daniel's eyes narrowed. His fingers picked up the paper napkin he had previously unfolded onto his lap. He tapped the corner of his mouth with it, and he let Nolan have his comic relief as he raised one eyebrow. "Perhaps, on this world, manners are a secondary requirement, my un-traveled friend."

The laughing caught the attention of the large-bosomed lady who was filing her nails behind the counter, when Daniel lifted his hand to signal her over. He watched as she moved from behind the bar, thinking she fit right into this retro establishment. She wasn't a large woman, at least in height, and she managed to cram the 30 extra pounds she carried into jeans she should have thrown out ten years earlier. The high heel shoes helped with the height to width proportion, but someone should have told her horizontal stripes on a shirt aren't flattering on a heavyset woman, notwithstanding the amount of cleavage stretching the material.

"Something I can help you with?" The woman's eyes danced across Daniel for a moment before she turned her thick-lashed gaze toward Nolan.

Nolan's chuckle stopped awkwardly when he realized the woman was talking to his face, but the eyes were furtively glancing at his crotch under the table.

The small oval nametag on her shirt matched the sign on the front picture window of the restaurant. "We could use a drink, Lucille," Daniel said as he saved his younger traveling companion from the awkward moment.

"Beer—a jug of draft," Nolan managed.

"Sure sweetness." Not being in a hurry, her eyes lingered on Nolan a few moments longer. "We have a custom in these parts. All the people who stop over just have to have their picture taken with *Fuzzy*."

"What is—Fuzzy?" Daniel had a curious look on his face.

Lucille giggled and both men shrank back in their seats, thinking the jiggling breasts might escape the confines of the skin-tight top. "No, Silly. Not what—but who." Her long, red fingernails scratched across the table top before she lifted her hand. The index finger came up, pointing into the far apex of the room.

Both men turned, their gaze following the indicated direction to Fuzzy. The stuffed grizzly bear was at least 11 feet tall, standing on its hind legs with teeth bared in a ferocious snarl. Its reddish-brown fur was matted and thinning, as time stole more from the bear than the bullet having killed it, many years before. Beside the great beast that once wandered the forest, was a large cork board covered in polaroid snapshots. Above the board was a colorful sign – *Fuzzy's Friends*.

"I think we'll need a few more beers to work our way up to that," Daniel said while winking at the woman.

"Sure, Sugar," she answered back. On her last word, her lips were left slightly open akin to Marilyn Monroe. She spun her weight expertly on one high heel before strutting back to the bar.

Daniel's eyes followed her stroll and he grumbled, "She does not look any better going than coming, my young friend."

They both broke into laughter, and it eased the underlying stress they both felt. Tension comes from many sources, and for Nolan, the source was the unknown. The pressure Daniel felt came from a different place. The stress visible on his face came from what he *did* know.

By the time Lucille came back with the jug of draft, they had finished eating. She slid the two glasses onto the table, right beside the frosted pitcher. Crossing her arms, she leaned over with her elbows resting on the table, causing her breasts to be pushed out in a way that would have her arrested in some States. Daniel thought it was not possible for any more flesh to peek out of the low-cut top, but he was wrong.

"I think I saw you two fellows here last year."

Daniel poured the beers. "You must have us mistaken for someone else," he replied with a polite smile.

Her upper teeth protruded too far as she smiled back. "I'm sure it was you two. C'mon—you remember. We had the big fuss at the beginning of the tourist season last year. Those two loads of young off-roaders ripped up the town with their Jeeps. Josh Kennedy finally had enough and came out with just three things: his underpants, that old shotgun of his and plenty of attitude. Needless to say…"

Daniel took a drink of his beer, seeing Nolan was already pouring himself a second as the woman went about recounting the entire history of the town in miniscule detail. He watched her lips. Incredibly, they didn't miss a beat as they blabbed on and on while she barely stopped to take a breath. The words blended together until all he heard was a monotone drone.

The woman gave no quarter. "And Jim Beatty, the poor man who owns the hardware store over yonder, he woke up one morning, and his wife was just gone. No one really knows where. She was a pretty thing and had the largest collection of shoes. When she came from Tacoma, she brought all the shoes with her. I have no idea why, but she wore high heels almost every day, even though they got caught in the plank sidewalk so many times." She looked down at the blank stares of the two men. "Where was I? Right. So, we figured she ran off with some young stud. She always was gawking at the hiking legs of those young college guys when they came to the store looking for…"

Neither of the two men had talked about religion. They didn't know if the other believed in Christ, Buddha, Mohammad, ancient gods of old or no god at all, but when Lucille was distracted away from them by the creak of the far door, as it opened, they both said a thankful, silent prayer to whichever god saved them.

Lucille straightened up from the table while her fingers fixed a stray wisp of colored, platinum hair. Her gaze centered on the three young, muscular men now entering the restaurant. In a distracted voice, she said, "Give me a shout if you two want another jug of draft." Her eyes were intent on the hunt and honed in on the three men in their early twenties. Not giving Daniel or Nolan a second thought, she walked over to welcome the younger men into her establishment.

Nolan and Daniel had been alone in the restaurant until the three newcomers entered, and now, as Lucille moved the newcomers over to a table on the far side, the booth they occupied was quiet again. They both sipped their beer until Daniel broke the silence, speaking just above a whisper, "In the morning, we will need to leave. We need to hide in the woods for several days."

Nolan slouched in the wooden bench seat. "I'm not going with you."

"What do you mean? We have discussed this. More people will come from Kaezzar to investigate what happened to their squad. When they find them dead, they will not be amused."

Nolan's fingers toyed with the glass of beer as his eyes looked into the amber liquid. "I'll be fine."

"You don't know who you are dealing with, Nolan." Daniel's voice came across again in a soft, persuasive tone. "Reconsider."

His body stayed calm in the relaxed slouch, but when Nolan's eyes lifted, they had a cold edge to them. His words came through tight lips. "Correct. I don't know who I'm dealing with, and that big unknown is *you*. You've explained much, except you left out who you are and what motivates you to be here with me. You don't seem the type of man who steps outside without a purpose. I don't know what your purpose is—just it isn't necessarily *my* purpose. I'm my own man, and I'll not follow anyone on a blind whim. There are always good guys and bad guys, and so far, I've gone along with the assumption the three strangers back at the station house wore black hats, but tell me—what color hat do *you* wear?"

Daniel's face was strained. Knowing this was a critical moment, he needed to make a decision. He didn't know if Nolan was ready for this, but the time had come for Daniel to *shit or get off the pot*. "Very well, my eager, young friend. My name is Daniel Barrymore Dupuis, but then the name itself is not that important. After all, a man is known by his deeds and not the name he holds as a birth rite. That rings true for what I call—a real man—one who lives life to the fullest with an unquenchable passion. So, tell me, Nolan Harrison, are you such a man? The man who would hear this story would be of that mold. It could be a new beginning for one who could absorb the implications and importance of what I am about to say." He cocked his head to the side. "Granted, it would be a beginning fraught with sorrow, but it would also have the exultation of life at every turn. Such moments make the beauty of this area and the awe of the mountains, pale in comparison. For some this is the fuel feeding their life blood. For others—let's just say the peace and quiet of an oblivious life suit them very well. Such people put their head in the sand and avoid the richness life can provide."

Nolan listened to Daniel and noted the look of honesty in his intense eyes. That, in itself, compelled him to continue listening.

Daniel put an arm up on the back of the bench, keeping his gaze locked on Nolan. "Where does Nolan Harrison fit in? Does he have a fire in his heart to match the potential in his mind, or does he return to a long and uneventful life in that little station house? In time, you would die, probably at a ripe old age. The chiseled letters in your tombstone would eventually fade, then it would be as if you never existed. The only thing remaining of you would be doubt, wondering if you made the correct decision, years ago on a cool night in the small town of Neilton."

"Don't bury me yet, old man. Tell me more."

Daniel saw Nolan's face had a bemused look, causing his tone to change with the smile forming on his rugged face. "Knowledge is power, Nolan. I have been wary of telling you too much. I knew, at some point, I would need to tell you more, and then you would need to decide on your course of action." His eyes met Nolan's. "Just remember, you asked me to tell you." He paused for a moment, giving Nolan another chance to back out.

Nolan didn't respond, allowing Daniel to continue.

"What I tell you will probably again bring some disbelief to your mind, but once you work through that, it will most assuredly bring depression to your heart. It is not a fairy tale with a happy ending. In fact, the ending could be quite final for humankind." Daniel tried to smile through his darkened mood. Although I have painted a dark picture, the places I will describe to you are those where a man really could make a difference—a real man!" He dwelled on the last word as his fingers balled into a tight, white-knuckled fist. "So, you shall learn why I am here, Nolan, but then you will have some decisions to make. Do you go back to your little station house in the forest where you think you will live out an uneventful and unmemorable life? Or do you take that chance that you—" His hand turned over and his index finger stretched out to point at Nolan "—could make a difference?"

Daniel took pride in the fact he never lost his composure, yet this time he had. His strong feelings about what had to be done fueled his emotions. He brought himself back down, slowing his breaths, and as he leaned back into the bench seat, his fingers clasped around the cold beer glass.

Nolan was surprised at the response he just heard. It wasn't the words themselves, but the passion Daniel spoke with. Whatever was on Daniel's mind began with a commitment in his heart. This type of passion was the difference between a lunatic and a hero—and everyone loves a hero. "I want to hear your story, but I don't see where I could possibly fit in. You also said human kind was at risk. Surely, I alone couldn't make such a difference whereby the plight of mankind hangs in the balance."

Crackles of loud laughter brought their attention back to the surroundings in the little restaurant. Lucille was sitting at the table with the three younger men who were now seated across the room, already finishing their second jug of beer. The taller, red-headed man seemed the obnoxious sort, obviously controlling the conversation and bragging of his exploits as a hiker. As if this wasn't enough to impress the woman who was over twice his age, he emphasized this wasn't a casual sport for them. They were professional, extreme hikers, and this was their life.

Daniel gestured to the opposite corner of the room. "It will be quieter over there. Interested?"

Nolan followed the direction of Daniel's gaze, and it brought his attention to a shoddy, old, dimly-lit pool table. They both rose to their feet, and Daniel looked over to Lucille and caught her eye by lifting the empty jug of beer. Lucille made an involuntary frown but complied with Daniel's request as she scurried to the bar.

Big Red also frowned with irritation. He didn't like having his place at the center of attention interrupted. He yelled over to Daniel. "Well, aren't we in a god damn hurry! You think you own this place, old man!"

Nolan was already at the pool table when Daniel turned to the three hikers who were all now hurling insults focused on Daniel's austere appearance. Daniel dealt with the likes of these fellows often enough, and he knew their brains were being driven by an overabundance of testosterone from testicles actually much smaller than they bragged. Daniel gave them an icy stare. He didn't waste any more of his energy on them and turned to the pool table where Nolan was racking the balls.

Nolan selected a pool cue, rolling it on the felt covered slate. The green hue of the felt matched the windows on the tacky tiffany lamp overtop of the table. He was thinking about what Daniel had said. In some ways, the older man said much with the emotion of his voice and the intensity he held in his eyes. At the same time, he said nothing other than riddles about humankind and a life he considered better than what Nolan had at the station house.

There was a loud *crack* as the cue ball pummeled the colored balls, sending them careening around the cushions.

Daniel watched the balls decelerate as he spoke. "The world I come from is very different from this one. It is called Crann Bith, and on its surface is a large city called Bailemor. That is where I live, and it is where I call home."

The yellow one-ball disappeared off the table into a side pocket.

"Looks like I'm *solids*." Nolan leaned over the cue with an experienced eye as he lined up the six-ball. "Hmmm, and I thought you were from Kaezzar." The tip of his cue struck cleanly, and the green ball was knocked efficiently into the end pocket.

Daniel's eyes grew wide momentarily before narrowing. "I am not from Kaezzar. The people from Kaezzar are our mortal enemies. They have been for many, many centuries. Therein lies the problem. You see, we have been at war for as far back as our history recounts."

"Why are you at war? What could possibly cause any civilization to be at war for an eternity?" Nolan's eyes were already on the seven-ball as he lined it up.

"Human instinct."

The maroon ball rattled the hole but teetered in. Nolan was walking around the table deciding on his next shot. "I don't understand."

"In certain respects, we are not different from any other forms of life in the Athar. We all have a natural survival instinct, and as such, we do a lot of things, but primarily we eat, sleep and fornicate. We survive so our species survives."

"That is understood, but how does it relate to this war you speak of?"

Daniel's face was shrouded in shadow. "Not all humans are the same, and we are very different from the Kaezzarites. You saw they had the ability to throw an energy burst. All Kaezzarites can do that. You also saw me use my energy shield. The people of Crann Bith all have the ability to shield themselves."

"You fight because you have different abilities?"

"Indirectly."

"To a point, I understand, Daniel. On this world, we have many wars, and they're usually based in differences in religion or politics, but they don't last centuries."

"Our situation is not so simple. The difference between the two peoples is a constant and does not change as would politics or religion. The constant I speak of is our DNA coding. Ninety-five per cent of the DNA Earth humans have is un-coded. Only five per cent actually defines clearly who you are and how you function. People from Kaezzar have a higher degree of coding. This difference defines their psychic ability to move energy. Now the people from my home world also have additional DNA definition, but it is slightly different from the Kaezzarites, and you see it visibly in that we can shield ourselves. However, unlike the Kaezzarites, we do not have the ability to throw the energy field from our bodies."

Nolan interrupted, "What does that have to do with survival?"

"The answer lies in how the two different DNAs interact. If the two DNAs reside in the same body, they compete for survival. They create enzymes which attempt to destroy the competing DNA strands. The end result, and it might not be complete for several generations, is the psychic DNA coding is destroyed, and the powers are lost."

Nolan's logical process kicked in. "Like the people of Earth."

"Yes, Nolan. Earthlings are descendants of the greater castes of humans who have occupied the Athar from the dawn of time."

Nolan was struggling with the enormity of the revelation and moved himself to the safety of the game. He bent over the cue, lining up the four-ball, but his hands were shaking, and the tip whiffed the white ball, sending it skipping to the side.

"There are more than Kaezzarites and Bailemorians out there," Daniel said. "As I have told you, there are many inhabited planes of reality in the Athar. The Kaezzarites are from the ancient caste of Toltec, and there are many Toltec worlds in the Athar. My caste is called Celtae, and we also occupy quite a chunk of the Athar, but there is also a third ancient caste known as the Anasazi. They have a smaller population, and are more obscure." Daniel watched Nolan straighten himself, seeing the look in the younger man's eyes was one of disbelief. "Remember, you asked me to tell you," Daniel whispered.

"Your shot."

"What?"

"You need to hit *stripes*. It's your shot."

The older man leaned over the table and nestled comfortably behind the cue. He supported the polished wood in a curled finger instead of the crook between the finger and thumb. He lined up a sky-blue eye over the cue and slowly struck the white ball toward the 13-ball.

"If we're descendants of these great castes, why aren't they here? Why is there no evidence and why did they leave?" Nolan's questions blurted out, one after the other.

The 13-ball finally trickled into the far pocket, and Daniel moved to line up the next shot. "Of course, there is evidence. Humans choose to ignore what they do not understand. You are not so different in your passion for war. That is why you have not discovered the secret of un-coded DNA or the unknown function of the brain or the relationship between psychic energy and *hopping* through the Athar."

"Hopping?" Nolan's confusion grew.

"Hopping is just a slang word for transposition. That would be the power that all humans of the three old castes have to transport themselves from one plane of the Athar to another. That is how I came here shortly thereafter followed by the three men who killed your friend. That is also how other Kaezzarites will come here to kill you if you do not come with me in the morning," Daniel explained.

Nolan kept a neutral appearance underlying the shock and confusion he was feeling. He shook his head. "I don't buy all of that. There must be some solid evidence from Earth's mystical forefathers."

Daniel hit the white ball ever so slowly. It seemed to take forever, but the targeted 12-ball finally tipped into the side pocket. "Every time your scientists discover something new in this field, their focus changes to how it can be used as a weapon. Albert Einstein was close to solving the whole puzzle, but your humanity turned it into an atomic bomb." Daniel stopped at the far end of the table, directly opposite from Nolan. "There are significant amounts of evidence Earthlings, because of their vanity, have a difficult time believing. You have a logical mind, so think about it. Did you know the great pyramid in Egypt actually has eight edges, each cut with a precision difficult to attain even with today's technology? Yet the Egyptian masons, 43 centuries ago, accomplished the feat. Did they do this without any assistance?" Do you really think the Inca's just woke up one morning and decided they would paddle across the Atlantic Ocean in canoes?" he scoffed. "And I assume you think Atlantis was just whimsical folklore."

Nolan's jaw dropped, looking at the older man. "Atlantis? Are you trying to freaking tell me…"

"Are you two amateurs going to finish your game, or just talk all night long!" Big Red slurred while his breath stank intensely of liquor. His two friends were right behind him, and they brought their liquor bottle with them, having moved on from the jugs of draft. The obnoxious trio caught Daniel and Nolan unawares. That irritated Daniel even more than the rudeness Big Red displayed.

"This is a private game. We will let you know when we are done, and the table will be yours at that point, not before," Daniel said.

Nolan listened with clenched teeth as he tried to hold back his own anger. He saw Daniel subtly shift his feet for better balance. There were no ulterior motives of softness or persuasion in Daniel's voice. Some people can be convinced, some can be coerced, but some people just need to be told, plain and simple. The blue steel in Daniel's eyes matched the direct tone of his voice. Clearly, Big Red had been told.

Big Red's eyebrows rose while creases formed across his brow. It had been some time since anyone stood up to him and even longer for a person of Daniel's age. He was wavering until he heard the voice of one of his friends behind him. "You gonna take that shit from him?"

Lucille didn't know what to do with herself. She finally went back behind the bar and set about cleaning glasses in her nervousness.

Daniel's gaze moved from her to the three drunkards who were inching closer. Nolan flipped the pool cue in his hands so the heavy side was up—baseball style. He glared a warning at the two in the rear as he slapped the cue into his palm.

"Who the hell do you think you are?" Big Red needed to save face, and the liquor was inspiring him. "An old man isn't going to get in my way! God dammit! Look at me! I'm one of the best hikers around. Tomorrow, me and my buddies are going to go north. No path or trail—I mean straight north over hills and mountains and through any other god damn thing getting in our way! That's the test, old man. Beating the piss out of you now is just a warm-up."

On the last spittle covered word, Big Red lunged forward, throwing a punch at Daniel's head, but Daniel wasn't there. He slid to his right, and his hand flashed out. The wrinkled fingers locked on a nerve on Big Red's wrist as it slashed by. He turned his hand over and pulled downward, pushing the drunkard's own hand into the small of his back. Daniel pinched with his fingers, and the bigger man howled, as his nerve sent spasms of pain up his arm.

Daniel wasn't finished. He put his other hand on Big Red's shoulder while his fingers dug into the nerve he knew was there. The bigger man howled even louder as he was brought to his knees with his hand pulled awkwardly behind him.

One of Big Red's friends rushed forward to slam into Daniel, but the older man, who was bent over, thrust his foot out horizontally and to the side, crushing into the foolish man's gut. Gasping for air and holding his torso, the second of Daniel's victims fell prone on the wooden plank floor. It only took a few seconds to play out, but two of the three brigands were out of commission.

The third of the trio let reason win over misconceived bravery and stood down as he watched Nolan continue to slap the cue into his palm.

"I warned you, did I not? But you went ahead and took a hasty course of action." Daniel spoke into Big Red's ear while his fingers were still locked on his shoulder and wrist. Since you have taken the trouble to cause this foolish situation you are now in, let's at least make it a learning lesson."

Big Red's howls turned to whimpers as the pain in his arm was replaced by numbness. He was totally subdued and in Daniel's power.

"First, you need to understand appearances can be deceiving. Never underestimate your enemy. Second, someone once told me a very important rule. Never throw the first blow, but make sure you get in the *last* blow. Third, the same man told me if you do throw the first blow, make sure it *is* the last blow." Daniel pushed Big Red forward, watching him fall over onto his face. "Think over those simple lessons while your arm comes back to life. The nerve damage is not permanent, and you should be just fine for your jaunt in the morning."

Daniel calmed himself. "With the distraction, I am not in the mood to finish the game, Nolan. Best we move on."

"If you're finished." Nolan gave a sarcastic reply through his smile.

The two men weaved through the arms and legs on the floor, making their way to the front door of the restaurant. Lucille had her back pressed up against the far wall behind the bar as they passed. She was going to point to Fuzzy, but thought better of it.

Daniel slapped a five-dollar-bill on the shiny, lacquered surface of the bar. "Send them a jug of beer Lucille." His request came through a warm smile.

It was just after midnight, and the town was quiet with only the noises from the forest wildlife in the distance as they walked back to Simmons Bed and Breakfast.

The serenity was broken as Daniel said, "So did you learn something tonight?"

Nolan waited for his yawn to subside and chomped his jaw a couple of times. "I learned many things, but not all. I learned you can handle yourself—and I learned you suck at pool," he said with a chuckle. Nolan looked up at the stars in the night sky. "For the rest, there's always tomorrow."

Chapter 6

There was a sharp knock on the door of Julian's office. He closed the file he was reviewing before placing it back in the lower drawer of the expensive desk he sat behind. Almost all the furniture in the ten stories of the Watch Command Center was standard issue, but he swindled this desk from a fellow in the appropriations office, who had tax liabilities he knew details of. He ran his fingers along the wide, black, leather border running the perimeter of the opulent desk. A satisfied smile was on his lips as he continued his daydream. It focused on the power offered from a position with leverage that, more often than not, infatuated his mind.

The knock repeated a second time.

Julian pressed in the lock on the drawer, making sure it was secure, then slid the keys into his pocket. "Enter!" he said in a loud, crisp voice.

The door swept open and two tall soldiers of Watch Command entered. They stood at attention, waiting for Julian to acknowledge them.

Julian's fingers played with his beard as his eyes inspected the unusual, off-world clothes the two communication runners wore. One had just come from the place called Earth, and the other would be replacing him within the hour. To him, it was a wonder, with all the modern technology they developed in Kaezzar that no one had yet found a way to communicate through the Athar. The only method of transmitting information back and forth was to use these runners. To make matters even more disruptive, the same runner couldn't go back and forth quickly. Hopping through the Athar took an abundance of energy, and it had to be replenished before a person could take a second hop. The time between hops was different for different people, but two hours was the norm. Runners were tested and selected based on this ability to replenish their energy. Candidates became runners if they could hop within an acceptance margin of an hour and a half.

Julian knew Ensign Morten just came back from Earth, but he hadn't previously met the other man. Whenever he met someone for the first time, he made a point of setting an impression in the other's mind. As such, he didn't offer them the seats on the other side of the desk.

"Ensign Morton—your report please," Julian coaxed.

Morton kept his chin high and his body at attention as he began his report. "Red Squad, under the command of Captain Enriques, arrived at Marker 23-1127-4 at 9:42 in the evening. Standard procedures were followed to secure the target site."

"Go on." Julian rubbed his hands together as he listened.

"The target area consisted of two structures. One was a small living accommodation, and the other was a storage building approximately the same size. There was a motorized vehicle used for flight on a landing pad, but it hadn't been used for at least 12 hours. The near perimeter was heavily wooded, difficult terrain, and an initial view of the far perimeter would indicate it was similar, although there were mountains in the background." Morton added.

"Stop," Julian said in a low voice. "Your report is ambiguous— 'initial view' and 'would indicate,' don't have a sense of accuracy to them."

Ensign Morton began to perspire. He chose his words carefully. "It was dark, Commander. The terrain was difficult, and limited time was available to accomplish the first report."

Julian rocked back in the black, leather chair as he gave a wide smile to Ensign Morton. "Ensign, in the future, when you report to me, use only clearly definitive words. If I hear you use words such as 'I think,' 'might have,' 'possibly' or 'would indicate,' again, I will break you out of the Watch so far, the only communicating you'll be doing is as a waiter telling a cook what kind of fried fish some greasy customer ordered! Understood?"

"Ye…Ye…Yes, Commander."

Julian rolled his chair closer to his desk. "Excellent! Were you able to secure an energy source?"

"Yes Sir. They have electrical energy readily available. Lieutenant Moore was able to rewire the radio, and our weapons were charged within two hours of our arrival," Morten responded.

Julian shook his head. This is another inefficiency you would have thought someone would have solved by now. In Kaezzar, we have all the advanced weapons, but we cannot hop with any form of additional energy. Significant amounts of local secondary energy will disrupt a pureblood's molecules, such that when he redefines himself at the tail end of the hop, he would be unrecognizable and quite dead. It means every hop has to include an energy officer who is highly trained in both natural and synthesized sources of energy. "Very well, Ensign. So, what happened to

Green Squad?"

"Green Squad is dead, Commander. One had his head split open. The other two received fatal knife wounds. There was also a dead scull. He was an Earthman who appeared—no—who worked at the structure we secured. Green Squad was found in the forest while the scull was carefully laid out on a table in the building."

Julian tapped his fingers lightly on his desk. It was a subconscious habit performed when his mind was awash in thought. Inside he was fuming. *Sculls killing Toltec soldiers!* Just hearing the word *sculls* put a look of bitter rancor on his face. Sculls was the general term used for humans who didn't have any psychic ability. Even though they were descended from the pureblood races, he thought of them as little better than farm animals. *Someone is going to pay dearly for this,* he thought. In that instant, his general disdain for sculls turned to a focused hatred for Earthlings.

"Who killed them?" Julian asked.

Morton was careful not to tell him he didn't know. "The dead scull was named John Baines. When we searched the premises, we found two identification cards in the aircraft. One belonged to Baines, the other belonged to a scull named Nolan Harrison." He stepped forward, placing the small ID card on the desk top.

"Continue, Ensign," Julian mumbled as he inspected the card, engraining the face into his memory. Across the top of the card, it read - *United States Department of Forestry.*

"The two sculls who were stationed at the building were caretakers of the forest. They couldn't have killed the members of the squad by themselves. We searched the area, and there were two sets of tracks leading away to the north. We didn't proceed further without additional orders." Ensign Morten slapped his hands against his sides and raised his chin even higher with his report now finished.

Julian looked up and waggled his finger at the other officer. "Ensign Mellanson." He recalled the name now. "Give these orders to Captain Enriques. I want him to maintain his cover and capture the two men. I don't want them killed."

Mellanson nodded his response. "Commander, from what Ensign Morten has told me, the terrain is difficult. We could do much better with an experienced tracker."

His hand rubbed his chin as he thought through the names he knew, then snapped his fingers. "This is good," Julian said through a chuckle. "I will arrange for Drew Sherman to meet you on the hop platform at 6:00 a.m."

"With all due respect, Commander, Drew Sherman retired from the Watch service over a year ago," Ensign Mellanson stated.

Julian ignored the young Ensign. "Morten, this is a secure operation. You are quarantined to the building, and you will not speak of this mission outside of this room. Dismissed!"

The two men could not salute and turn to the door fast enough. "Mellanson!" Julian shouted.

The Young officer turned back quickly, "Yes, Commander."

The devious smile was on Julian's face again. "Remember, I know Ensign Morten quite well. I don't know who the shit you are. Good luck."

The door closed, and Julian was alone with his thoughts. He couldn't help but believe somehow the Celtae were behind this. *Opportunity always lies in someone else's misfortune, and I'll be damned if anyone else is going to get to it before me.*

He placed his finger on the pressure sensitive keyboard on his desk, and the screen sitting on the corner of his desk came to life. Julian entered his password and dug into the electronic files for his private phone listings. His fingers rubbed his chin. "There it is—Drew Sherman," he mumbled.

He pressed a key to put the system in *Voice Mode,* and he said, "Dial." There were several electronic clicks, then audible ring tones—four of them. The answering machine clicked in, but before it disconnected, Julian said, "Abort," and the computer cut off the call. "Computer—redial."

The process repeated, but this time after the third ring a voice came on the audio. "Screw off!" The words were followed by the crash of the receiver at the other end of the connection.

Julian chuckled as he looked at the clock on his wall. It was 4:40 a.m. "Computer, redial."

Once again, the gruff voice came on the audio, "I don't know who the hell you…"

Leaning close to the speaker, he raised his voice, "This is Julian Morenz, Commander of the Watch, Fourth Sector. I wouldn't be waking you this early if it wasn't important."

Drew switched to video mode, so they could see each other. "I'm retired, so you have no business with me."

Julian looked at the round face he saw on the screen. It had a long scar down the left jawbone, which you could see through the thin cover of graying beard. His eyes were dark, not only with color, but with the memories and guilt of deeds gone by. "Mr. Sherman, we have an emergency at Watch Command. We could use a man of your skills, notwithstanding your retirement."

"Who the hell do you think you are? I don't care what you command. I finished with the Watch and their ways a while back. I'm done."

Julian forced a smile. "I was hoping I could convince you to come out of retirement for just a few days. We're hopping a runner at 6:00 a.m. and I was optimistic I could convince you to join him. You see, we've lost some of ours on an exploratory mission, and we need a highly-skilled tracker to find the culprits. You're the best in that regard." Julian tasted bile through the smile. He hated this patronizing shit.

"Go to the next guy on the list."

Julian watched the monitor and saw Drew's hand about to hit the cancel button, when he said, "How's your father, Mr. Sherman?"

Drew's face froze. "My father is not so well. He needs a kidney transplant, but thankfully, he's near the top of the list. He'll be okay if he gets the organ soon."

Julian tilted his head, but he made sure Drew could see his eyes. Even under the long feminine lashes, he exuded evil. "I heard he was ill, but I'm sure it will work out fine. It's just, when you hear these stories about the politics of the list, where people lobby for support in our wonderful State government, often the next thing you know, the list gets shuffled. I really hope that doesn't happen to your father when he's so close to the top."

It didn't take Drew long to consider his options. He had been one of these leaches for many years, so he understood the underlying message— loud and clear. "I'll be at the hop platform at 6:00 a.m." he said through clenched teeth. Then the monitor went blank.

Julian leaned back in his chair with his feet up on the desk. His fingers were intertwined happily as he closed his eyes, taking in the euphoric joy of the moment.

Chapter 7

Nolan awoke to the light prattle of rain on the small window illuminating the room. From the sound, he knew the rain was soft—somewhere between a light drizzle and a mist. He enjoyed this time, lying in bed and listening to the calming sound that was unchanged since the dawn of life. He loved to hear the natural sounds of rain, wind and thunder. They reminded him of his mortality and also the fleetingness of time, feeding his desire for knowledge and wisdom.

Smiling, subconsciously, he wondered which path he was going down now. He'd not told Daniel, but he was absolutely enthralled by the tales the mysterious stranger told and the possibilities therein. Other worlds and other castes of humans who had powers beyond what he could ever have imagined, dragged him toward adventure. However, he still needed to take care, as Daniel hadn't clearly defined where he fit into the Athar. If Daniel's point was to kill him, it would have already happened. Daniel had skills and abilities hidden by the guise he portrayed. There was much more to the strange Celtae, who was now his traveling partner and, it would seem, soon to be mentor. He took a deep breath and sighed, resigning himself to the fact the balance between his search for knowledge and his need to use wisdom, was teetering well to one side. Daniel laid out a puzzle of humanity, but there were pieces missing. Nolan needed to discover the missing pieces, and fit them in. The knowledge would surely lead to wisdom.

Nolan's philosophical musings were broken by the sound of footfalls in the hallway, coming toward the pine-paneled door of the room. The harmony of the rain faded into the background as he slid himself up to a sitting position in case he needed to move quickly. The black, wrought-iron handle was at least 30 years old, but in spite of the traces of rust, it still worked well. The door was pushed open and Daniel, shrouded in his leather hat and knee length coat, both sopping wet, entered under the archway.

"You have slept late, so I brought you something to eat," Daniel said as he threw Nolan a sandwich wrapped in wax paper. "By the way, Lucille said to say, 'hello.'" He gave Nolan an amusing grin as he removed his coat and hat, transferring them to the coat rack to dry out.

Turning his wrist, Nolan looked at his watch. It was already 9:30 a.m. It was unusual for him to sleep this late, but then again, the last two days were anything but normal. The smell of bacon wafted up to Nolan's nose, making his mouth water. He tore open the wax covering before sinking his teeth into the toasted sandwich. He looked over at Daniel who was sitting on the other pine-board bed, and Nolan's words came between hungry bites. "So where are we going today?"

"It is time to begin your training. We need to find a place where we can have some peace and quiet for a few days. I was hoping you had a suggestion since you know this area better than I," Daniel replied.

As Nolan chewed, he thought of the land. He replayed in his mind the bird's eye view of the forest and mountains he had flown over so many times. His recollection wandered the lush terrain, considering different spots, reassessing each time until he saw the cabin.

The small, quaint room Daniel and he sat in came back into focus. "There's a cabin about 12 miles northeast of this location. It's higher in the mountains, and the terrain around it is difficult. We'd have to leave soon to be there by night fall."

"Is the cabin empty and isolated?"

"Very few know of it," Nolan said. "I do because I've seen it in my fly-overs. It belonged to Josh Macgregor who was a little kooky and mostly kept to himself. Not many even knew he was out there, and that was the way he liked it. We used to see smoke from the cabin on a regular basis, but there was a spell of two weeks where it was missing. When we went down to investigate, all we found was the rank smell of Josh who died days earlier of a stroke. After we pulled him out, we boarded up the cabin. I would think it has been untouched since, and that was eleven months ago."

"Excellent," Daniel responded. "Best we pack up our things here, then pick up some additional supplies on our way out of town. By the way, you need to pay Simmons for the night's accommodation. My credit on this world is somewhat nonexistent."

Nolan rolled his eyes as he hopped out of bed. "Why does that not surprise me?" he mumbled.

It didn't take them long to wash up, pack their things, and with a thank you to Mr. Simmons, they made their way onto Spruce Street. Nolan enjoyed the mist on his face, but he needed wet weather gear to keep him dry. He looked over at Daniel who looked like a throwback from some old spaghetti-western movie. His narrow face was stoic under the wide-brimmed hat pulled low over his eyes. Small droplets of rain accumulated on the brim, then dripped down onto the faded leather coat. Although Daniel looked quite the sight, Nolan noted the hat and overcoat were effective in keeping him dry.

They were walking diagonally across the street when, in the distance, they saw Big Red and his two companions stride out of Lucille's restaurant. They glanced over, but only for a moment. They pulled their packs to their backs and with a degree of haste, headed north out of town toward the main trail.

In the distance, Nolan saw the three hikers plunge into the bush, making short work of the first steep incline before disappearing over the treed rise. "Christ, they're quick. I wonder if they keep to that pace for long."

Daniel turned to him with bright eyes and a smirk on his face, "I hope so."

Nolan furrowed his eyebrows, returning his own look of curiosity, but he didn't bother to ask. The hikers were gone—history.

They made several trips back and forth between the general store and the hardware store. First, they picked up larger packs. Next, they packed them with canned and freeze-dried food and, finally, a few additional items to stock the cabin. Nolan was still loading the last few items into his pack when Daniel, who was looking out the front window of the hardware store, suddenly dropped to a squat with his hand held in the air.

The older man hissed out his name, "Nolan! Come here quickly."

Hearing the tone in his voice, Nolan immediately squatted beside Daniel. Daniel's arm came down, and he pointed toward the south end of town. "Look."

Pressing his face up against the glass so he could see the end of Spruce Street, Nolan asked, "Who are they?"

The older man had his eyes trained on the nine men who appeared at the far end of town. "They are Kaezzarites, and they're here much earlier than I expected. Damn!"

One man seemed to be giving instructions to the others, with his hand pointing in different directions around the town. Two of the men remained at the far end of the road. One began walking around the western perimeter of the buildings while the other six strode slowly down the sidewalk. It was a direction that would quickly take the strangers by their present location.

Daniel turned in his squat, leaning his back against the window. "You saw the weapons?"

Their dress and general appearance did remind Nolan of the three killers at the station house, and under their coats, he saw the flash of a silver muzzle. "They have some type of shoulder-slung rifle under their coats."

Daniel looked intense. "Good eyes, Young Nolan." He put his hand on Nolan's shoulder. "We are outnumbered and outgunned. Simple logic tells me this is not the time for a fight. Consequently, it is absolutely imperative we leave this town in stealth. We need them to stay here for a time looking for us, so we can steal off without them on our tails."

With His eyes still locked on the Kaezzarites, Nolan nodded his head up and down in agreement. They were still quite a way down the road, but they were getting closer.

"Very well—follow me." Daniel leapt to his feet, and three long strides brought him face to face with Jim Beattie who was behind the cash register.

"Do you have a back door?" Daniel questioned as he struggled to maintain a cordial smile.

Behind his bifocal glasses, Jim Beattie pulled his eyes up from the newspaper. "Ahhh, sure, but I just use it for…"

"Show us the way, Sir." Daniel urged.

Jim Beattie was a simple man, and in his life, he learned not to worry unnecessarily about things, nor did he try to figure people out. He had seen some strange folk come through over the many years he owned the store, and he wasn't about to try to understand the strangely attired man— especially now in the middle of his morning newspaper. He just raised his hand, pointing to the small hallway leading to the back, then turned his eyes back to page four.

The two men slung their packs before heading down the short, dark hallway. Daniel cracked open the metal door and peered south. With no one in sight, they spilled out the door into the brush-infested, back alley. The forest had slowly worked its way back toward the buildings, reclaiming the alley with brush, sword ferns and tree sprouts. It was broken only by the two lines of patchy gravel running across the back of the shops.

Daniel hastened toward the gravel, using it as a pathway. "We need to be invisible. Keep to the gravel until we arrive at the ravine. We will follow it up to the old train station."

Nolan nodded his understanding as he followed Daniel down the pathway. The rain had become heavier, and Nolan was thankful he purchased the poncho-style, gray raincoat. They trod quickly down the alley, pausing for a moment as they passed each narrow cross-alley running up between the shops. At each, once they saw it was clear, they would scoot across.

It only took them a few minutes to reach the 12-foot-deep ravine bisecting the town. Stretching from the foothills behind them, it wound through the town and was lost from sight through the railway trestle in the distance. Earlier, during the spring, the ravine would've been full of fast flowing water, but now the stream was only two feet deep and slow moving. The water meandered around rocks and larger boulders, pushed here by the powerful, annual rush of spring-time water. The grass, liverwort and ferns were even thicker here than in the forest. Nutrients from the mountains were washed down with the cold mountain water, finding every crevice and hole to provide a perfect environment for the cycle of life.

Using the sporadic rocks as handholds, Daniel and Nolan climbed and half-slid down the ravine. Other rocks in the stream were excellent stepping stones, allowing them to travel the short distance to the small concrete-based bridge supporting Spruce Street.

Daniel crawled up the side of the ravine, again using the rocks to step and pull himself up so just his cold, blue eyes were visible under the sodden brim of his hat. As he spied down the sidewalk, it was just in time to see three of the strangers pass into Lucille's restaurant. Two others were continuing their slow, searching progress down the sidewalk toward his concealed location. That accounted for five of the six men who began the walk down the sidewalk. *Where was the last man?* Without moving his head, his eyes scanned the street through the now beating rain. Finally, he saw him. His furtive form was moving up one of the lanes toward the west side of town.

Daniel slid back down the ravine. "We only have a few minutes to find a concealed location. Move quickly and be invisible." Daniel jumped into the stream and began moving quickly with the flow of water, westwards toward the trestle.

The deep-cut ravine veered slightly to the south, and both men trudged as best they could through the knee-high water. Nolan realized what Daniel was doing. If they walked along the intermittent rocks, they would have been slower. If they walked through the vegetation, their tracks would have been visible. They needed to get far enough around the bend to let the geography obscure them before the two Kaezzarites reached the bridge.

It's too late, Nolan thought. His thigh muscles were aching with the exertion of trying to run through the water. *We're taking too long, and any minute I'm going to feel a bullet or an energy blast in my back.*

Finally, Daniel's face turned, and he hissed, "Now!" after which he threw himself prone against the sharply angled side of the ravine.

Nolan followed Daniel's lead, tasting dirt, as his face pressed into the moist soil. He knew there was some risk here. Through the brush, he could still see the back corner of the bridge. From that vantage point, he knew they were not completely concealed to someone who had sharp eyes and keen senses. He prayed the Kaezzarites on the bridge were short sighted, and the rain would not let up. As they waited, their chests pounded into the soil with every thunderous beat of their hearts.

Nolan held his breath as a man came into view not 40 yards from his position. His heart leapt into his throat, as the man walked around the side of the bridge and slipped down the embankment. The man was still visible from the waist up. He pulled back his coat and brought his weapon up into view. He looked under the bridge, then his eyes turned to the ground, looking for any type of tracks. Suddenly, the man lifted his head to peer directly at their partially concealed location while he panned his weapon back and forth across the ravine.

Freaking hell, Nolan thought. *We're done.* He had the urge to bolt up and run for it. However, he was frozen, and to his surprise, it was fear, not prudence, holding him there.

The second man appeared at the top of the bridge and hollered down to his partner. The man in the ravine shook himself much like a dog would with droplets of water flying in his futile effort to keep dry. He was wet, and it compelled him to discontinue his search down the ravine. He scampered back up the embankment, and the two men disappeared from view as they continued to their posting at the north end of town.

It was still cool in the late morning, but it didn't stop Nolan from heavily perspiring under the raincoat. He felt Daniel's hand on his shoulder, helping him to his feet.

Daniel was quick and to the point. "This side is clear," he whispered as his finger pointed to the bridge. The hand came back in front of Nolan's face, holding up two fingers. "There are still two men unaccounted for somewhere on this side of town. If they see us, head north as best you can. I will try to meet up with you there."

Nolan nodded his understanding, and he realized he'd been doing a lot of that around Daniel. They continued their trek down the stream with Daniel in the lead, keeping his eyes ahead and looking for any signs of the other two unaccounted for men. They kept a careful pace as they proceeded through the 60 yards to the train trestle. The ravine was deeper here at about 30 feet. Both men froze themselves to the thick beams supporting the trestle above.

The rain had reduced back to a slight drizzle as Daniel said to Nolan, "I will climb up first. When I signal you to come, follow quickly."

Nolan was getting frustrated. All he could do was nod again. He watched with some dismay as Daniel showed exceptional dexterity and strength while making his way up the 30-foot climb. Using the old timbers making up the ancient bridge, and, from time to time, a rock outcropping from the sheer face of the ravine, Daniel worked his way higher and higher.

Once directly under the trestle, Daniel slid his head around the side of a vertical support beam. First, he twisted his neck to look south. The rusty railway tracks veered to the right and out of sight, while the shoddy laneway veered to the left. At the far end of the lane, some four hundred yards away, was one of the Kaezzarites pacing back and forth where he monitored his corner of the town's perimeter.

Daniel slung himself to the right, so he could view the northwest corner of town. The old, unused railway line made a straight-line north until it was lost in the trees and undergrowth. The laneway swept to the right, making a loop around the far end of town, where it was lost to view behind the corner house. Here, the last Kaezzarite was pacing the northwest corner of the perimeter.

Waving his hand under him, Daniel motioned Nolan to begin his climb. His eyes looked back and forth from one Kaezzarite to the other as each of them paced back and forth lazily across the far ends of the laneway. Daniel kept his head lower when the Kaezzarite's pacing brought his place of hiding into their peripheral view, since either of them could pick up any small movement. They were out of sync with each other with the man at the south end pacing faster.

Daniel felt Nolan's fingers tap his leg and he heard Nolan's words through heavy breaths. "I'm here."

"Keep your head down until I tell you, but when I do, we need to move quickly. We are going to go north on the railway tracks. Just make sure your footfalls are on the ties since we need to be invisible," Daniel whispered.

Inside, Nolan laughed as he caught himself about to nod, but then realizing Daniel wasn't even looking at him. Nolan was hanging prone with his arms and legs slung around a thick wooden trestle. His strength held him there, but he hoped Daniel would make the call soon. His raincoat was slick as it was, but after lying face first in the mud of the ravine, he felt his hold slowly slipping.

Daniel watched and waited as each of the Kaezzarites continued their casual pace back and forth across their ends of the laneway, and the man at the south end was catching up. He was waiting for the point in time when both men would be facing away from their position on the bridge.

Only a few more minutes, Daniel thought. He turned his head back and forth. *On the next turn keep going,* he silently implored both of the armed men.

"Now!" Daniel stressed his voice. Both men were facing toward the town, but as Daniel had been watching, he knew they only had two minutes. If they weren't out of sight by then, they would be easily seen by both armed men.

Nolan had been able to hang on to the trestle by applying brute muscle power to his grip, but it was sapping his energy. Consequently, he was grateful to follow Daniel's lead up to the railway tracks, even though he still felt every movement in his aching limbs.

As soon as his feet hit the railway ties, Daniel slapped Nolan's shoulder, then pointed north down the railway tracks, "Run," he urged through clenched teeth.

They both ran down the tracks with Nolan in the lead and their feet hitting only every third tie. It was going to be close. Daniel kept his eyes on the man to the north. He would be the one to turn first. Damn! He's stopped. *We are done,* Daniel thought, putting even more speed into his surprisingly nimble legs.

The Kaezzarite at the north end tilted his head to the side as he tried to hear the communication coming through his earpiece. He turned around, facing south, as his finger pressed the earpiece further into his ear, trying to hear the static-garbled message. As he lifted his head and looked at the bridge, he didn't notice the sword ferns along the overgrown railway tracks were waving—nor was he alert enough to realize this odd, as the morning rain fell vertically with the lack of any wind.

Chapter 8

Adrian Korlis was the Chief of Watch Operations for the state city of Kaezzar. As such, he carried ultimate responsibility for identifying and investigating all unknown activities in the Athar, including unauthorized transpositions.

Korlis was a burly, barrel-chested man who was a veteran of both the Kaezzar military wing and Watch Command. As a military strike team captain, he was decorated several times in the long-standing war with the Celtae. The quick *in and out* strikes monopolizing the aggression between the two castes gave him a wealth of field experience and the accompanying scars. He gained a no-nonsense, get-the-job-done notoriety from his peers that was noticed by his superiors and the senators who pulled their strings. That was until his left lower leg was blown off by a touch mine.

Fortunately for Korlis, those in the ruling party who noticed him remembered his exploits. This was particularly true for one senator whom Korlis saved a year earlier when the senator was kidnapped by a militant faction of Celtae. When this same senator heard of Korlis's loss, he lobbied the president of Kaezzar who also happened to be the senator's father-in-law. Before Korlis even learned to walk on the artificial limb, he was appointed chief of Watch Command, arguably the most powerful organization within the state-run, socialist government. The appointment also put Korlis directly in a position blocking Julian Morenz's self-inspired career path.

Julian sat in Korlis's board room, tapping his fingers lightly on the table as he half-listened to the reports from each sector commander during the weekly operations review. His boredom started from the first moment Cherez, who was the sector two commander, gave his report. Shipping hops—hops for vacationers—the odd military exercise—the information was painfully as mundane as the spartan board room they occupied. Thankfully, they kept the temperature cool otherwise, surely, he would have fallen asleep.

In any case, Julian had other subjects on his mind. The previous night,

Ensign Mellanson reported in at 11:00 p.m. as directed. There was nothing of consequence in his report other than Drew Sherman tracking Nolan Harrison and his unknown accomplice to a small town called Neilton. They made the trek in record time, so it seemed Drew Sherman's tracking skills had not collected any rust. Perhaps they were even crisper, now tuned as a result of the smoldering anger he must feel toward Julian. He could not contain the smug grin, picturing the sweat on Sherman's round face as he thrashed an angry path through the Earthen brush.

"Your report, Commander Morenz." Korlis's raspy voice pulled Julian from his self-centered thoughts.

Julian surveyed the other eleven sector commanders, and his eyes finally turned to Korlis at the head of the table. *It was the chair he should be sitting in,* Julian thought as his fingers pulled open the file folder in front of him.

Julian gave a concise and organized report providing statistics on the activity in his sector during the past week. He always gave detailed reports, and this was no different except he made the effort to keep his voice even more monotone than usual. After all, he didn't want to bring any unwanted attention his way. Today, he wanted his report to be the most mundane of all, finishing his report with a per functionary, "Any questions?"

Although Julian asked all the listeners, it was only Korlis who ever asked for details, and this occurred only rarely. Korlis had his head tilted down, fingers rubbing back and forth across his forehead as he read a copy of the report in front of him. After a few minutes, his eyes turned up to Julian. "There was a rumor of a disturbance in sector four."

Julian had acquired the skill of deception over his 35 years while leveraging his way up the career ladder. He put it into effect now, keeping a casual, calm demeanor—even a trace of a smile—while his asshole was puckering so tight, he thought he would suck the cushion up from the chair he sat in. He shifted in the chair and put both forearms on the table while intertwining his fingers. "There was a small disturbance in sector four, Chief Korlis. It appeared to be some rogue explorer passing through the quadrant, and as procedure dictates, we sent a squad to investigate. The evidence to date agrees with our initial assumption. It really isn't even worth our time, but our watch is thorough, so we'll complete the investigation. If anything meaningful comes of it, I'll bring it to your attention at that point." He pressed his lips closed and formed a wider smile notwithstanding the increasing pressure on his sphincter.

Korlis's gaze lingered on Julian for a few moments, looking him up and down, and then it mercifully shifted to Julian's left. "Commander Sanchez—

sector five's report, if you please."

Julian almost shit himself, as his sphincter muscle relaxed. He leaned his head down while he closed his folder, feeling the redness flush over his face. Thoughts were racing through his mind. *Who leaked the information? Korlis has someone inside my organization! Shit! Who is it? Even more care and diligence will be required from here on in. Nolan Harrison was an opportunity—his opportunity—not Korlis's!*

The ops review dragged on for another uninspired hour until, finally, they were released. Julian marched out the door as he looked at the time. He would have to hurry to make his appointment across the city, so he paused in his office for only a moment to drop off his file before scurrying to the elevator. As Julian touched the button for the ground floor, he heard the mechanical *click* of the brakes disengaging followed by the *whoosh* of air, as the ballast bag sealing the car to the shaft, deflated. The controlled seepage of air put the elevator in a calculated drop down eight floors. As the elevator passed the third floor, the computer controls inflated the ballast bag at a prescribed rate so the car came to a smooth stop. With a barely noticeable bump against the spring-loaded overtravel bumpers, the elevator was at the ground floor.

Julian was out the doors before they were fully open. Swiping his identity card, there was an audible click before his hips pressed through the unlocked turnstile. Nodding to the armed security guard at his post, he pushed open the large, glass door marking the border of Watch Command, whereby he found himself in the crisp summer air of Kaezzar. Inhaling deeply, he looked up at the dull, yellow sky which was a constant, blanketing the city during daytime hours.

He hastened down the stairs, looking both left and right, contemplating what he considered to be one of the most prolific streets in all of the Athar. Citizens Boulevard was 40 yards across and covered in purple and gray square stones. The man-made stones were each one-foot-square and perfectly aligned with each other along the boulevard's entire 20-mile length in each direction from the central intersection of the city.

Bordering each side of the boulevard were stone buildings. The ornate architecture utilized primarily round columns, curved buttresses and elaborately carved lintels and sills, giving each building a personality unto itself. The city zoning office gave quite a bit of liberty to the buildings structure, but they were not so liberal with the color schemes. These were approved or changed by the zoning committee, so the general aesthetic appearance remained in tune with the theme of the city or, at least, the theme the Senate Council fostered. Consequently, pastel colors were the norm in the central core of the city where Watch Command was located.

Julian veered right, coming off the bottom stair before heading for the Eye of the city, just 40 paces south of his present location. This was the central intersection where Veterans Parkway crossed Citizens Boulevard. Veterans Parkway was as awesome a sight as The Boulevard. It was equally as wide, and the pastel blue and gray stones ran 30 miles in each direction from the Eye. Both roads were so well known that, when Kaezzarites talked of the Boulevard or the Parkway, further description was not required.

Julian took a moment as he reached the Eye. Rush hour hadn't yet set in, so only a few primarily uniformed citizens walked the roadway. The only other movement was a bus having stopped in the bus lane running along either edge of the thoroughfare. Other than this form of public transportation, only emergency or state police vehicles were allowed on the streets of Kaezzar.

Along with the buses, the citizens of Kaezzar used the elaborate system of underground trains known as *MagTraks*. Knowing he had to hurry, Julian didn't waste any more time as he stepped onto the escalator taking him down to the MagTrak levels.

The configuration of any MagTrak line across the city was consistent with a grouping of four tunnels—two on top of two. The top two tunnels were the short mag and the emergency mag. The two lower tunnels were the commercial shipping mag and the long mag. The short and long hop mags were the primary source of public transportation available to Kaezzarites. The short MagTrak utilized slower trains making stops at every station along the line. These vehicles ran at up to 40 miles an hour, making it approximately five minutes between any stops. Faster, aerodynamic mags, cutting through the tunnel air at 150 miles an hour, used the long hop tunnel. These trains only stopped at every twentieth station along lines that were perfectly smooth and provided banked turns, so maximum speed could be utilized. This led to an exceptionally efficient system of public transportation, whereby anyone using a combination of overland buses, short and long mags could move from one location to any other location in the city within 30 minutes.

The remaining two tunnels in each line were the emergency MagTrak and the commercial shipping MagTrak. Julian had only been in the emergency tunnel twice. Once as a child he broke his leg, and the second embarrassing trip was when he accidentally shot himself in the hand while he was a military cadet. In that instance, he bought off his roommate to lie about the circumstances of the shooting, and it watered down the stupidity fueling the incident. But the incident, along with the permanent nerve damage to his hand, still resulted in a quick discharge from the cadets. It also resulted in a cursory letter of reference beginning his career in Watch Command.

The commercial shipping tunnel was the last one in each grouping. Each building or business had a group of service elevators connecting down to this level. Julian used his security access to visit this level often. It was a city unto itself, thriving with hawkers and merchants who felt a level of comfort amongst the laughter and camaraderie bustling through the working-class citizens of Kaezzar. On the other hand, Julian enjoyed the irony. These people built this city with their sweat. They received only a meager income and a frugal living space, yet they seemed happy. Viewing them rejuvenated Julian, reminding him he would never accept this level of life. Even more importantly, it reminded him of the lack of control these people had over their existence. The visits motivated Julian, spurring him on in his quest for power that was the basis of his being.

Today, Julian wasn't going to the shipping tunnel. His business was elsewhere, leading him to the third level where the Boulevard short hop mag was just coming into the station. The electricity coursing through the linear motor in the locomotive vibrated through the air, resulting in a background of light, static noise. The compressed air pushing ahead of it furled loose wafts of clothing and disheveled, unkempt hair.

The doors to the front, first-class car opened, and Julian showed the attendant his security clearance. The man smiled, and having seen him often, he stepped aside to allow the commander access to the plush, black seats. The static sound began to build as the brakes were released. The acceleration pushed Julian back in his seat as the electromagnets powered up, and the contact brushes transferred the energy into forward momentum. The acceleration and deceleration cycle occurred three more times before Julian arrived at his stop in Education Square. It was a district occupied primarily by the state university and the 40 thousand students enrolled in all types of educational programs.

Disembarking from the MagTrak, Julian moved up the three flights of escalator to street level where he cut down a back road off the Boulevard. He continued past several buildings before turning down an even smaller laneway. Here, he had a secret apartment in one of the university residency buildings that he often used as a safe house. A few times, he had hidden operatives here, but he also used it as his own personal getaway, when needed.

This was only the first of Julian's two destinations this afternoon. He needed to change into civilian clothes since a watch commander attracted attention at the best of times, and he would look even more out of place when he reached his final destination across the city in the Commercial District. Once Julian was dressed in the drab, less than eye catching, civilian clothing, complete with a wide hat, he retraced his path to the MagTraks. However, this time he took the escalators down to the second level, where he found a worn seat in the standard class car of the long hop mag servicing the commercial ring.

The City of Kaezzar could be best described as a city of rings. The entire city was the shape of a 40-by-60-mile oval, with the Boulevard and Parkway bisected the oval along the two center lines of the city. Other MagTrak lines ran in oblongs circling around the city at different radial distances from the Eye. The commercial ring was well named, as along its entire length, the land was zoned only for shops, restaurants, entertainment establishments and service businesses. Similarly, there were other MagTraks that carried passengers through the residential, military, industrial, and agricultural sectors of the city.

Julian felt the MagTrak accelerate to 150 miles an hour, then decelerate three times before he was at his stop in the northwest quadrant along the commercial ring. He pulled the hat low over his eyes and stepped onto the escalator moving to street level, nervously looking behind him every few seconds. The long shadows of the buildings covered the street of gray stones. This lower-class district was marked by a plethora of neon signs and colorful advertisements, coaxing people to the main drag.

Keeping his head tilted down, Julian crossed the road and stopped in front of a men's clothing store. He looked into the picture window, but his eyes focused on the glass as he dissected the reflection of the other side of the street. His examination lasted a few minutes, and he moved on only after he was satisfied no one was following him. His feet moved him quickly back in a southward direction until he hit the seedy side street he searched for. Looking furtively behind him one more time, he scurried along the street until he came to a glass door that was painted black. The picture window beside the door had the same black treatment that provided a contrasting background for the yellow letters stenciled on the smooth surface. It read, – *Porters Club for Gentlemen*.

Julian pulled the door open, slipping a ten-cort bill into the doorman's hand before slithering into the barely lit club. Two women were dancing on the low stage where their naked flesh was lit by the kaleidoscope of colors from the stage lights. The dancing didn't match the music playing through the speakers, but the exclusively male clientele didn't seem to notice. Their alcohol-laden eyes were more interested in the seemingly impossible geometrical positions the women moved their bodies into.

Behind the bar, along the far wall, the bald bartender spied Julian and put down the glass he was cleaning. There was an almost imperceptible nod of his chin, and his hand came across his chest followed by a finger nonchalantly pointing to the curtain hanging over the entrance to the hallway in the back of the establishment. Keeping the motion fluid, his hand came up, spreading all the digits, signaling a "five" to the disguised commander. The bartender was careful, but the patrons were so fixated on the show of flesh, he could have yelled, "Booth Five!" across the room without anyone noticing.

Julian chose a path around the fringe of the room, keeping his left shoulder to the wall after again looking back to the door to ensure he didn't have any unwanted shadows. Having reached the curtain, he slipped it aside, and his pupils dilated to the brighter light, revealing the seedy condition of the hallway. The floorboards creaked under his step as he counted down the numbers over the small alcoves along the length of the hallway. Once he reached alcove five, he took one last look behind him before sliding back the curtain and stepping through.

Luis Ortez was expecting Julian, but he still shot up nervously from behind the small round table. His plump features glowed in the red light from the single incandescent tube hanging from the side wall.

Julian removed his hat. "Good afternoon, Citizen Ortez. I hope your day has gone well."

Ortez had a confused uncomfortable look on his face. "Yes...Yes, Commander. My day is fine," he stammered.

Julian had a twinge of anger visible in his eyes, notwithstanding the dim red light, as he looked at the overweight man. He whispered through clenched teeth, "Do I look like I'm wearing a uniform? I told you before. When we meet—when we talk on the phone, or anytime you refer to me, you'll address me as *Citizen Cool*—understood?"

A sheen of sweat appeared on Ortez's face, highlighting the nervous twitch at the left corner of his mouth. "Yes," He managed.

"Yes—what?"

"Yes, Citizen Cool," Ortez acquiesced.

Citizen Cool bent and slid behind the table before settling into the billowy cushions of the curved booth. He bobbed up and down several times before coming to rest. The cushions were filled with water for the enjoyment of the patrons who, for 20-cort, could bring a girl of their choosing back here for an inspired ride on the high seas. Ortez slid in behind the table from the other end of the booth, and the ride began all over again.

They waited for the undulations to stop before Citizen Cool said, "Luis, what do you have for me today?"

Ortez tilted sideways, as his hand was having difficulty getting into the pocket of his trousers under his overhanging belly. After a few seconds of contortions, he pulled out a small plastic tube and placed it on the table. "The discs in the tube are all the communications Adrian Korlis has had in the past week. The blue discs are the communications from his home, and the green ones are from his office line."

"Is there anything incriminating on the discs?" An evil, optimistic look lit up Citizen Cool's eyes.

"Nothing Citizen. I have been monitoring Korlis's communications for three months now. He is squeaky clean."

Citizen Cool took off his hat and placed it on the table, choosing his words carefully. "Luis, have I not been your friend? When you were in desperate straits and needed money, was I not there to help you? When you got into trouble with the woman—no, let me rephrase that—with the young girl in the hotel, wasn't I there again to help you?"

Ortez squirmed on the cushion. *He knew Commander Morenz—shit— Citizen Cool—had him by the balls. Damn! He was so screwed up, the watch commander had him correcting himself in his thoughts!* He never knew the girl was under age, but considering how much he drank, he couldn't remember most of that night. It was only a few days later, when Citizen Cool showed him the graphic pictures, that the lapses were filled in.

"Citizen Cool, are you certain you are the only one who has a copy of the pictures?"

"Of course, Luis." Citizen Cool lifted a finger while turning his eyes up to the ceiling. "You see, this is exactly what I mean. I'm doing you a very big favor by keeping those pictures in my safe possession. You have an excellent job as a field supervisor for the State Communications Department—one that would disappear if someone unscrupulous came across the pictures. Now, I've asked you only for a very little favor in return. I've asked you to tap into a few communication lines and find me a skeleton."

Ortez's mouth began to twitch faster as he blurted out, "There's nothing there! I have looked and looked and looked!" His voice blended into the loud music from the bar in the background.

"Everyone has skeletons somewhere, Luis. Some are better hidden, and to find them, you have to look harder. *You* need to look harder," Citizen Cool urged.

Ortez put his elbows on the table before leaning his forehead against his palms. "How did I get myself into this mess? What fate brought the girl to me that night?" he mumbled.

Citizen Cool watched the man, thinking how pathetic he was. *It wasn't fate, my asinine friend. I picked you from eight candidates in the communications department, and your profile brought the highest probability of success, or, from your perspective—failure. Everything went as planned. You had your night of passion. The girl received her 100-cort, and I secured my mole on a leash.*

"Do you have access to his computers through the optical communication lines?" Citizen Cool asked.

"Yes, of course."

"Keep monitoring communications, but pull everything off his computer. You might find something there. I want you back here with something solid in three days," Citizen Cool stated with a finality that told Ortez he could leave.

Ortez didn't waste time. He slid quickly out from behind the table and made a bee line for the curtain.

Citizen Cool watched the ditch impressed in the cushion by Ortez's ass, slowly rise, as the water pressure equalized. "Be a good fellow, Luis, and give the bartender 80-cort. Tell him 20 are for him, and 60 are for Selena to make her way back here. You've severely stressed me, and I need to relax before I go home"

Ortez bit his lip and nodded. He didn't look up, but he knew the smug look the evil man would have on his face. His feet couldn't move him fast enough as he rushed out of the room and down the hall.

Chapter 9

Nolan and Daniel ran at a good pace for some 300 yards before they slowed to a more casual gait. They kept their careful footfalls confined to the wooden railway ties as they watched for the invading rot from the encroaching forest.

They both looked back at intervals, and it was Daniel who finally said, "It appears none follow. We can walk, but keep your eyes on the ties and your ears to the forest. We don't need any more surprises today."

Nolan took Daniel's direction and slowed to a walk while his chest was still pressing in and out with heavy breaths. "Freaking hell. That was too close." He ran his fingers through his hair that was soaked with a mixture of sweat and the rain still falling in a light drizzle. "I sure hope you know what you're doing," he mumbled.

Slowing to let Nolan come beside him, Daniel looked at the younger man with empathy. However, the gaze was short lived with the knowledge the Kaezzarites were so close on their heels. "It is a much over used saying, but, truly, sometimes our destiny is written for us. Such is your life right now, my young friend."

Nolan turned and looked up at the taller man, ready to come back with one of his typical quips. He hoped he gave the illusion he was still in some semblance of control. Although one door was open wide while others seemed to be closed tight, he still liked to think it was his choice to not bust down one of the barred paths. However, when he heard Daniel call him friend, along with the sincere look in his eyes, he softened. He realized, in that moment, Daniel was truly becoming his friend—a friend who saved his life twice now. The only word coming to Nolan's lips was a quiet, "Thanks."

Tilting his head down, Daniel looked at the wealth of vegetation surrounding them. The old timbers and stone base of the railway line had kept the invasion of different shades of green and brown foliage from completely over running the path they followed. Rolling his eyes upward, he noticed the thicker overhead canopy forming a tunnel-like cover which diffused the light rain into a mist. The sun, now high overhead, sent rays of light into the canopy, finding the smallest of openings to burst through to the forest floor. Daniel provided an ironic grin as he saw the rays of light pass through the mist-laden air, forming the tiniest of rainbows. He wished Nolan could remain as innocent as the heavenly apparition before them, but he knew, although the young Earthman had learned and seen much in the last two days, there was so much more Nolan would need to prepare for.

Daniel turned back to Nolan with a reassuring smile. "You said you know your way to the cabin east of here."

"I can get us there," Nolan replied. "The road will be easier if we stay on the tracks. They veer northeast just beyond the upcoming bend." He pointed his finger through the mist.

Daniel slapped Nolan on the shoulder, "Very good."

Walking on for a few minutes, the silence was broken intermittently by the singing of birds overhead. Sure enough, the tracks turned, and they were heading in a direction toward the cabin still some 11 miles away. With the midday excitement, Nolan had tucked his many unanswered questions into the locked recesses of his mind, but one in particular was rushing to the fore front. "Tell me about Atlantis."

Daniel brushed a low hanging branch from his path. "Atlantis was the initial colony which arose after the first exploratory mission by the Ionians. Here, on Earth, Atlantis is remembered as folklore and better considered so, but truth be told, it was a very real city."

"The Ionians?"

"You recall I told you the Celtae, Toltec and Anasazi were the three pureblood castes fathering humanity as you know it. Well, originally there were seven pureblood castes. The three I mentioned are the three remaining. Unfortunately, war brings death, and continuous unabated war brings annihilation. The other four castes have disappeared from existence, and the Ionians were one of those castes."

Nolan's curiosity grew. "Why did the Ionians come to Earth, and where are they now?"

"The Athar, as we know it, is no different from Earth as seen by your explorers of centuries ago. At that time, the Earth was seen as endless by many civilizations. Explorers were sent out, and once their flags were staked into the ground, colonies followed shortly thereafter. The Athar is no different except it truly is endless, while the Earthen explorers eventually found this world has limits." Daniel wiped the moisture from his forehead as he continued. "Long ago, the seven pureblood races sent explorers out into the Athar, traveling to different planes as accessed by their more powerful minds. It was common for a colony to be established once a plane was secured. The Ionians took Earth as their own, and their colony was called Atlantis."

Nolan almost stumbled, as his toe hit a rock between the ties. Once he righted himself, he continued the flow of questions. "So, where are they?"

"They left." Daniel replied. "It was at a time when the war between the great castes was in its infancy, and some believed there could be a peaceful solution. They hoped a solution could be found, whereby the great races could live together. The Ionians led this line of thought and worked feverishly to find the elusive solution. They even invited the Kush, one of the other now extinct races, to form a sister colony on Earth, and they did so in the land you now call Britain."

"So, what happened?"

Daniel answered through smiling lips. "Ah, well another instinct took over. We humans have a need for love and companionship seen only in a few other species of life. So, it was inevitable men and women from the two castes would mingle, mate and bear children."

"And that is when the Earthen population began." Nolan finished the thought as he looked off into the mist. "We're the descendants of the great races, just without the higher-level psychic powers."

"Exactly," Daniel agreed.

"It still doesn't explain where they went. Some purebloods must have been left," Nolan probed.

"The war between the castes continued to escalate throughout the Athar. The fleeting harmony between the Ionians and the Kush was a threat to those who promoted aggression. More and more raids came to Earth, primarily against the higher castes, but also against the growing population of lower caste humans. Finally, there was an epic battle. Both the Ionians and Kush cities were attacked in great force by an alliance of Toltec and Celtae forces." Daniel lowered his head, pausing a moment before continuing. "The Ionians survived, but the Kush city was obliterated along with every living human within it, high caste or low."

Nolan's jaw was slack. The cruelty of humankind was not limited to only Earth, but unfortunately to many other planes of the Athar.

"The Ionians knew it was only a matter of time before another reinforced attack would come. The large population of humans were at risk, so they left," Daniel explained. "The Ionians were better engineers than fighters. They set demolitions at critical areas in their city. The resulting explosions destroyed every trace of their existence before they left this Earth. It was a similar story on other planes, but still the need for war was relentless and followed them. The weaker castes were hunted and killed until we heard of them no more."

"But didn't the Ionians and Kush also have higher level psychic abilities?" Nolan asked.

"Of course. That is what made them higher caste humans, but some psychic powers are better utilized for aggression than others. The power of the shield I have, the power of the energy burst possessed by the Toltec and even the ability the Anasazi have to teleport their bodies from one location to another, are all very effective tools in battle. The Ionians had the ability to move matter. It is the skill your world calls telekinesis. The Kush had the power of illusion, projecting holograms of themselves or other objects at will. Although these powers were amazing, they were less effective in the course of battle as was the Shang's ability to read minds or the Bantu's power to sense oncoming events. Consequently, there are now only three castes left."

Daniel held up his hand before Nolan could ask the next question, then squatted on his haunches in the underbrush. He inspected the path cutting across the railway tracks as he pulled up a few of the bent plants. Bringing the jagged broken ends of the stems closer, his eyes put them through a thorough inspection. Now, Nolan also saw it. The plants were beaten down over a localized area. The beaten path came from the south and cut directly north up into the foothills. He watched Daniel, whose eyes were downcast, walk back and forth through the area, stooping over occasionally to continue assessing the plants and soil.

Finding a tree on the fringe of the tracks, Nolan lowered himself into a sitting position with his back against the rough bark. Closing his eyes, he leaned his head back and wiped his moist brow. After a few moments, he heard Daniel lower himself and lean back against the same tree so their shoulders touched.

Without opening his eyes, Nolan said, "What do you think?"

"Three travelers, moving quickly. I am pretty sure it is Big Red and his two companions, and they are two to three hours ahead of us."

Nolan cocked his head, opening one eye to peer at the older man "We're continuing east to the cabin, aren't we?"

Daniel leaned his head back against the bark. "Yes, but we need some time. We need a diversion. Big Red is moving quickly as he foretold. The Kaezzarites will certainly have a difficult time catching up to them."

"Why the freaking hell would the Kaezzarites follow Big Red?"

"Because they think we are with them," Daniel replied with a coy grin on his thin lips.

Nolan sat forward while turning to look squarely at Daniel. "Cut to the chase. What aren't you telling me?"

"If you recall, I was up early this morning and had breakfast at Lucille's."

"Yes…Yes…" Nolan tried to hurry Daniel along.

"What I didn't tell you is I had breakfast with Big Red and his two companions. His arm was much better, and he forgot all about the night before once I told him breakfast was on your tab." Daniel twirled Nolan's credit card between his fingers. "On my way out, I whispered to Lucille that Big Red and I were now fine friends. In fact, we were so taken with each other, Big Red invited us to come with them on their excursion." Daniel explained.

Nolan broke into laughter. "You're a freaking evil, old man. You knew, within an hour, the whole town would know!"

"I consider myself a good judge of people." Daniel gave a sly wink.

They rested for another 15 minutes until the light rain thankfully abated, but unfortunately, it was replaced by increased humidity. They each pulled out a power bar to eat and made short work of them before rising and heading north, following Big Red's path.

"Don't worry about tracks now," Daniel said. "We want the Kaezzarites to see us."

Nolan nodded a response, noticing the terrain was now grading uphill. There were less and less spruces and maples and more and more hemlock and fir as they trekked further up into the foothills. They followed the path of Big Red and his two companions, and as Big Red stated, "He didn't veer away from difficult obstacles." Rather, he moved over the crags of rocks becoming predominant at this higher altitude. Between the warm sun spreading a wide path through the less dense vegetation and the soft, warm, east wind, their joints lost the dampness of the last few hours, making the trek more comfortable.

They came across a small clearing where it was obvious the trio in front of them stopped for a rest. The area's brush was crushed down, and in the center was a make shift fire pit where the red-hot embers were now parched white from the consuming flame.

Daniel turned to Nolan and asked. "Help me move two more rocks by the fire."

At first, Nolan wasn't sure what Daniel was up to, but it clicked when he saw the three larger rocks close by the fire pit. Clearly, they were seats used by the three men. "Got it," Nolan responded with a grin.

It didn't take them long to find two suitable rocks in the terrain, moving them next to the other rocks by the fire pit.

Daniel looked at his watch. "We need to continue on. It would be convenient if we could get to the cabin by 6:00 p.m."

Nolan pressed a hand into his pack and pulled out his wallet. "Wait a minute," he said. His fingers searched through the small plastic sleeves until he found what he searched for and pulled out his old military identification. Leaning over, he pushed it down between the rocks, partially concealing the card behind a clump of long grass.

"You learn quickly indeed," Daniel chuckled. "Now, let's move east. Keep to the rocks, and be invisible."

The pair of travelers pushed aside their weariness, knowing there were still two hours of hiking over what would now be tough, rocky terrain. Moving due east, they skirted the mountainside, keeping a close eye on their footholds. The sheer cliff drop-offs bordering their path did not deter them, nor did the precipices they climbed down. They worked together in the hope of arriving at the cabin by the forecasted time.

At one point, they came to a long, softly-rounded rock outcropping pushed up by glaciers from centuries before. The easier footing allowed Nolan to catch his breath. "Why do we need to get to the cabin by 6:00?"

"I need to send a message across the Athar."

"This might sound like a stupid question, but won't the Kaezzarites be able to see your message?"

Daniel stopped and turned to the younger traveler. "There are no stupid questions—only stupid people who do not ask questions." He put his hand on Nolan's far shoulder, turning him toward the panoramic view of the forest spread out before them. "Do you see the pond below?"

Nolan first gave a curious look to Daniel, then turned his searching gaze across the expanse below, seeing only miles and miles of forest. After several minutes he said, "No, I don't see a pond."

Daniel raised his left arm and pointed to the southeast. "Follow the direction of my arm. Do you see it now?"

Squinting one eye, Nolan spied down the length of Daniel's arm, taking a minute before seeing a tiny pond. It lay hidden within a thicket of spruces, surrounded by a river winding like a snake through the valley. "I see it now."

Daniel slapped his hand down on Nolan's shoulder and said, matter-of-factly, "There you go!" before walking away.

"What do you mean—there you freaking go?" Nolan replied as he ran to catch up to Daniel. "My signal through the Athar will be hidden in the background. The people I would send the message know where to look, and when to look. It helps that, at the same time I will send my message, there will be a large, daily transposition of workers to a mining colony in a nearby sector. The message will be caught up in their psychic wake and be invisible except to those who know to look for it," Daniel elaborated.

Nolan led the way as their passage inclined downward, off the large rock formation, back onto the angled mountainside. "It seems I don't know much at all about the Athar. What does it look like?"

"You have seen it. Tell me, do you dream about the stars?"

Nolan was surprised. "Yes, I dream about the stars often. Mind you, I'm not really sure it's a dream. It's more of a lucid state somewhere between a dream and reality."

Daniel nodded knowingly. "Those are not stars you are seeing. They are markers and activity in the Athar. All purebloods having a higher level of psychic ability can intuitively see the Athar in their mind. Some can see it better than others and are used as see'ers, but all have at least a basic ability. It's not dissimilar to your sense of where this cabin is. You have seen it before, and you know the forest, so you remember the way to it. It is intuitive."

"There it is"

"There's what?" Daniel had a confused look.

"The cabin," Nolan answered.

Daniel looked along the mountainside before them. "Where? I can't see the cabin any more than you could see the pond."

"Good! I wanted to make sure it wasn't just me," Nolan snickered.

Daniel lowered an eyebrow in a chastising glare.

Nolan nodded his chin forward, "There to the left in the forest of firs."

Squinting, Daniel finally saw the small cabin on a brief plateau which jutted out from the side of the mountain. Even from this distance, he could see the boarded windows on the log structure underneath the flat, angled roof. "I suppose it's better than spending the nights in the open air," he offered.

The short distance to the cabin was covered uneventfully. It was in a very small clearing in the midst of tall fir trees. The tree needles made a soft, reddish blanket, covering the ground so that even the most persistent of alpine plants would have a difficult time rooting. There was a second, smaller structure they assumed was a shack. Here, the door hung on an angle off the top hinge, creaking in the gentle wind always blowing through these higher reaches.

Daniel looked at his watch. "Nolan, it is almost 6:00. I need to prepare to send my message. Why don't you check the cabin, and I will be with you momentarily?"

Nolan's curiosity was at a high, so he wanted to keep Daniel within sight. Looking over Daniel's shoulder, he saw a rusty crowbar leaning against the wall. "I'll un-board the windows. It'll be nice to have some light in the place." Without waiting for a response, he walked past Daniel toward the crowbar and set about his work while keeping one eye on the older man.

Daniel moved to the center of the small clearing and pulled his watch off. He placed it on the ground in front of him. Removing his hat, he placed it to the side and set about searching through his pack. His fingers pulled out a conical object small enough to fit into the palm of his hand. Moving himself to a kneeling position, Daniel kept his eyes on the watch and placed both hands around the object. By now, Nolan had forgotten about the crowbar in his hands and was intent on the older man in the small clearing.

Daniel sat back on his haunches and closed his eyes. The green energy field came to life flickering around him, causing his features to become hazy in the electric glow.

Nolan wasn't sure he saw it the first time. The small points of light moving through the energy field became oriented, polarizing to the object in Daniel's hands, resulting in an instantaneous pulse of green radiance from the conical shape. It faded and the small points of polarized light moved even faster, shooting toward the cone. The second bright illumination convinced Nolan of what he saw. The pattern repeated and the conical object glittered with intensity a third and final time. This time, the energy field disappeared altogether. Daniel's body slumped to the side onto the bed of red needles. His glazed over eyes were open. His breaths were heavy.

Nolan broke from his position in a run but was stopped in his tracks. The air next to Daniel became distorted akin to the ripples made when a stone hits water. The ripples resonated out from the center, and the amplitude increased until Nolan could not see through the opaque, eight-foot-high oval having formed. Nolan's feet were frozen to the spot, and his mouth hung open, but his eyes were riveted on the distortion. It had peaked and was now beginning to fade. As it did, colors appeared and separated into form and shape. As the ripples ebbed, Nolan began to take involuntary backward steps. The distortion was gone and replaced by a vision of a man dressed in outfitter clothes. His dark countenance was highlighted by a hawk nose and jet-black hair pulled back in a tight ponytail.

Nolan's heel hit the low veranda of the cabin, causing him to fall backward, the result being his ass hitting hard against the wood boards. The vision turned as quick as lightning toward the noise, pulling a knife from his belt as his legs bent to a crouch.

Nolan's eyes opened wide in amazement. It wasn't a vision at all. The man was real!

Chapter 10

Julian was late. His hand, on the knob of his office door, paused as his face contorted into a wide, trembling yawn. He took longer than he should have with Selena, but the female's experienced fingers and lips had been quite a distraction. Once he finally left, he traveled to his apartment, catching a few hours of sleep before finding himself back at Watch Command. Not that he cared, but he was over an hour late for the next report from Earth.

With the yawn complete, he gave his head a quick tilt to the left, causing a soft audible crack. It cleared his memories and brought him back to the present. His hand turned and pressed the door open, revealing Ensigns Morten and Juarez scrambling to their feet and to attention.

"Good evening, gentlemen," Julian offered as he walked to the other side of his desk. There, he fell into his leather chair opposite to where the two young officers stood. The two men shifted awkwardly, their stance turning to follow Julian to where he now sat.

Juarez, being the runner just back from Earth, broke the awkward silence. "Ensign Juarez reporting, Sir!"

Julian's face contorted and vibrated as he tried to suppress a second yawn while waving his finger nonchalantly toward the two chairs opposite him. As the two men slid into the offered seats, Julian said, "I must say, I heard Red Squad was the elite of the elite when it came to field reconnaissance." Sliding his hand up onto the table, he tapped his fingernails in a repeating pattern on the shiny surface. "So far, I've been disappointed. Not so much by Red Squad but by the remaining squads if you're, in fact, the elite of the bunch," he concluded with a sarcastic smile.

"We're indeed getting closer to apprehending Nolan Harrison and the other man who is traveling with him, who we now know is named Daniel," Juarez stated.

Julian clapped his hands together as his head nodded up and down. "Amazing! Just amazing! Red Squad has been out in the field for a day, and we *now* know the first name of the one we search for."

"There's more, Sir."

Eyebrows tilting down, face darkening, Julian slammed a fist down on the table. "Out with it then! I'm tired and impatient!"

Both ensign's bodies jerked, as they were startled by the crack of the fist.

Ensign Juarez fumbled as he pushed the image across the table to the watch commander. "We've finished with our search of Neilton, and we know Harrison and this other man, Daniel, spent the night at a local boarding house. They also spent much of the evening at a local food outlet owned by a woman called Lucille. She told us Harrison and Daniel left in the morning with three other travelers, heading north through the mountains."

Julian squinted while examining the picture closely. "What's this then?"

"The three men in the picture are the ones Harrison and Daniel left Neilton with, and we know who they are. The big man with the red hair is Jeffrey Larmer. The other two are brothers—Nick and Robert Milton," Juarez responded.

"What's their connection? It can't be just pure chance they're in this small town." Julian mumbled, talking to himself as much as to the two young officers.

"On the contrary, Sir. Harrison and Daniel are both resourceful and dangerous. In fact, last night they had a physical altercation with the three men you see in the picture. The information from Lucille described how, in the morning, they put the confrontation behind them. Red Squad left the town and are following the five travelers who are moving quickly, but not very carefully. Drew Sherman sends the message, 'He will have no problem tracking them.'" Juarez wondered if the watch commander was still listening since Julian's head was bent so close over the photograph.

Julian brought a finger up, pointing toward the picture. "What's this— this creature?"

Juarez felt more comfortable. Knowledge is power, and power gave him some standing with Commander Morenz, even if it was likely to be short lived. "It's a creature native to the forests in the vicinity of the town. It's called a 'Fuzzy'. Apparently, they are quite ferocious and, as such, are difficult to catch. The sculls of the planet have a custom, whereby if they capture one of these Fuzzies, they kill it, stuff it and put it on display to view while they eat."

Julian finally came back into eye contact with Ensign Juarez, and his disdain for the Earthen version of sculls multiplied. "The Fuzzy looks dangerous." He pushed the photograph to the side, returning his focus to the topic of importance. "Anything else on Harrison or Daniel?"

"That's the extent of my report, Commander. I hope it has improved your opinion as you reflect on Red Squad and the other field soldiers who serve the Watch." Juarez met the commander's gaze.

Julian's eyes grew wide as the word "reflect" opened a deeper door in his mind. He snapped the picture back in front of himself as his other hand pulled a magnifying glass from the top drawer of his desk. Bobbing the lens up and down, he focused the magnified view through the round housing. The picture of the Fuzzy with the three men was taken against a corner window of the food establishment. It was distorted, but the large picture window reflected the remainder of the restaurant in the background. He panned the magnifying glass slowly across the picture, clucking with delight as he finally found the break he needed.

Julian's words came in quick spurts. "Juarez. You may go. But you are quarantined to the building. Go—go!"

Ensign Juarez jumped to his feet, then scampered out of the office.

Turning his attention to Ensign Morton, Julian continued his quick words. "When you leave here, the *first* thing you'll do is bring Sub-Commander Rankin back to me. *Then,* you'll report to Captain Enriquez on Earth, taking three fresh soldiers with you. I want a rotation every six hours—three men in and three men out. I want the team fresh and alert, and make sure all are aware of the danger from the Fuzzies!"

"Yes Commander!" Ensign Morton stood and saluted."

With a squint in one eye and the corners of his lips down turned, Julian pointed at the young ensign. "And tell Captain Enriquez, if he wants to remain a captain much longer, he best find Harrison and Daniel quickly!" His hand snapped to the left, pointing to the door. "Now go, man!"

Ensign Morten almost fell over the chair in his haste to remove himself from the room. The sounds of his boots hitting the tiled floor as he ran for Sub-Commander Rankin, could be heard receding even after the door slammed shut.

Julian sat alone with his thoughts bouncing back and forth in his mind. Something didn't seem right. *Why would the three men take Harrison and Daniel with them? Was it just coincidence, or were these three really sculls or Celtae operatives?*

Julian had difficulty believing people, purebloods or sculls, could be helpful without some ulterior motive. *No one does something for nothing, so what's in it for these three men?*

There was a sharp knock on the door. "Enter!" Julian shouted.

Sub-Commander Rankin's appearance was not crisp. Her shirt was twisted. Her hair, usually well kept, had wisps protruding from the side and back, while her usually pretty eyes were glazed and underlain with puffy skin.

Pointing her to a chair, Julian gave an irritated shake to his head. *Damn,* he thought. *Too much drugs, or maybe not enough drugs.*

Rankin sat, crossing one leg femininely over the other, and the motion gave Julian a glimpse of the despised high heel. "I apologize, Commander. Being under quarantine, I was sleeping in my office when Ensign Morten came for me."

Bitch, Julian thought as he smiled, pushing the picture over to her. "Have you seen this?"

She looked down. "No. It's the first I've seen of it."

A short wave of disappointment came over Julian. He was looking forward to chewing out the woman. Instead, he handed her the magnifying glass. "What do you see?"

"This creature—what is it?"

Julian loosened his wrist, moving his fingers in a circular motion. "It's a Fuzzy, but don't concern yourself with it. Look at the reflection in the left side of the plate glass."

She did exactly as Julian had done a few minutes before, bobbing the magnifying glass up and down as she focused in closely on the area Julian directed her to.

"It's fuzzy." She looked up for a minute, back pedaling "I'm sorry—not the creature. The reflected image is fuzzy," she said, then cackled nervously. Seeing his annoyance, she cut off the cackle almost before it began, returning her gaze to the picture. "There are booths along the other side of the room. They're all empty except one where two people are sitting. One is turned with his back to us, but the other, if you look closely, has blonde hair. However, the image isn't clear at all."

"I want this picture taken down to Photo-imaging. Tell them I want the man's face filtered and magnified."

"There's no one there at this hour, Sir."

"Don't you think I know that, Sub-Commander?" Julian emphasized the "Sub" in her title. "Why do I have to think for everyone around here? Show some initiative and wake someone up!"

She jolted up out of the chair and stood at attention. "Yes, Sir!"

Julian's lips formed into a wide, tight, satisfied smile. He noted she had jumped up even faster than either of the two ensigns had. "I'm going home to get some sleep. I want the report from Photo-imaging first thing in the morning." Not waiting for a response, he shooed her out, leaving him alone with his thoughts.

That's when the floor of the room seemed to jolt upward, knocking him out of his chair. After the initial blast wave, the building shook for several seconds, struggling to stay on its supports while absorbing the energy and transferring it deep into its reinforced footings.

As quickly as it came, the reverberations of the explosion ended. Julian had been through several terrorist attacks, but this one was the closest. He removed his hands from the back of his head, then lifted his head from the prone position he was in, with his stomach flat against the floor. He looked back and forth. His chair was on its side. The only other visible damage was a hairline crack on the far wall.

Julian smiled, and as he realized he was still alive, the smile turned into a laugh. The laugh became louder. He couldn't help but think of a running Sub-Commander Rankin, with high heels clicking in a quick rhythm against the white hallway tiles, as she tried to keep her balance. He turned onto his back holding his belly as the laughter intensified. He knew, even in the energy of the blast, she would continue her mission to Photo-imaging. He knew she wouldn't waiver even as the attack sirens sounded, one after the other, throughout the city, drowning out his hysteria.

Chapter 11

Transposition of a person through the Athar is one of those things looking easier than it really was. It consumed quite a bit of the person's internal store of energy—enough, in fact, so the person wouldn't be able to perform another transposition for at least an hour and a half. With that considered, there's always an element of danger when one hops into another psychic plane. There's no real way to see ahead or to know if the spot selected is safe or teeming with danger to face as soon as one's molecules reform.

There's a natural element of logical sense to all things in the infinite planes of the Athar. Consequently, it's not possible to reform in the middle of a tree, or ten thousand feet above the ground. A pureblood's psychic sense allows him to see the Athar and the markers within it. There are varying levels of skill, but if one knows where to look, a person can accurately hone in on the location. The intuitive ability is similar to a shark having a sense for blood and being able to find even a few drops from miles away. Once a pureblood senses a marker's location, he can place himself at the exact position, or a predetermined distance from it with due consideration for the topography of the land mass within the plane. The stranger who materialized in front of the cabin chose the former, and he was right on the mark, only a few feet from Daniel's position.

Nolan was improving his recovery time from shock. The unearthly event he just saw was added to his memory of the energy blast and the energy shield, but this time his jaw was not hanging so far in wonderment, nor was the urge to hyperventilate as strong. Reaching for the long crowbar, he wrapped his fingers around the cold, rusty metal. Tilting its direction, pointed into the deck board, he rose to his feet while never taking his eyes off the newcomer who had a definite exotic aura about him.

Taking a slow step forward, Nolan said, "Move away from him." He lifted the crowbar to a threatening position held across his body.

The dark stranger matched Nolan, pulling his knife up in front of himself. He warily sidestepped, crossing foot over foot until he blocked Nolan's line of sight to Daniel.

A shiver ran through Nolan as he considered the knife. It was no simple hunting knife he saw in the stranger's hand. It was 12 inches of smooth, metallic arc. The light-silver color along both edges indicated they were ground razor-sharp. There was a twin knife in the sheath hanging from the left side of the man's belt. From the worn appearance of the leather hilt, he surmised both blades were well used. In all, the man looked simple but efficient. *Danger.* That was the word echoing over and over through his mind as Nolan inched forward.

"Germaine, he is a friend. Stand down." The low raspy voice came from Daniel who was propped up on one elbow, his hair soaked with sweat.

The stranger's knife arm lowered several degrees when he heard Daniel's voice. He gave Nolan a dark, *move and I'll cut your throat* stare before back pedaling and dropping to one knee beside Daniel.

Dead eyes. That's what Nolan saw when the stranger locked his gaze. In the moment, through the stranger's cold guilt, he saw the pained gawk of death. It confused him. Keeping the crowbar at the ready, Nolan moved toward Daniel, his legs pent up like metal coils ready to spring at the stranger if need be.

Daniel saw Nolan's apprehension. "It's okay, Nolan. Germaine is a friend of mine—close enough a friend to trust him with my life. He is here because I called him."

Seeing Germaine sheath his knife and help Daniel to a sitting position, Nolan lowered the crowbar. The trembling through his body subsided as the adrenalin levels came back into equilibrium. Feeling more at ease but not yet devoid of all suspicion, Nolan covered the ground to Daniel, squatting beside him while keeping Germaine well within view.

"Germaine, this is Nolan," Daniel said as his voice began to recover.

Germaine was focused on Daniel and didn't lift his head. "You are a friend of Daniel's?"

"Yes, he's my friend, although I don't think he would trust me with his life just yet," Nolan quipped.

Germaine lifted his head. Thankfully, the eyes were softer, and an impassive smile momentarily crossed his lips. "It's good to meet you then." He held his hand out toward Nolan.

As Nolan pushed his hand forward, Germaine's hand slid up his forearm, and his fingers clasped just below the elbow. Nolan awkwardly clasped Germaine's own forearm, reciprocating what obviously was an off-world greeting.

"Okay, enough already." Daniel chuckled. His energy was coming back to him, and he made the effort to rise. With one hand on the ground, he tried to push himself up, but his balance teetered.

The arm clasp yanked apart abruptly as both Nolan and Germaine reached to catch Daniel. With one man supporting each arm, they raised the older man to his feet and moved him toward the cabin. Every few steps Daniel faltered in his weariness. Once at the fragile porch spotted with broken boards and popped nails, they placed Daniel in a wide-bottomed, wooden chair.

With a light chuckle showing his embarrassment, Daniel said, "It seems I need an hour or so to rest."

There was genuine caring in Germaine's eyes as he looked at Daniel. "I thought your days of adventure were over. This isn't what I expected you to be doing when you told me you retired," he said while putting a hand on the older man's shoulder.

"There is much for us to talk about, but that will have to wait until later. There is danger about so we need to secure this site first. What you need to know immediately is I would not be here if it was not of critical importance. We will need to stay here for several days—perhaps even a week. It could be made difficult since there are at least nine Kaezzarites on our trail."

"Kaezzarites, here!" Germaine hissed through clenched teeth, and his knuckles turned white as he instinctively grasped the shaft of his knife.

"I believe we have some time," Daniel said in a persuasive tone. "I sent them along a false path, and it should give us the time we need, but you need to back track, verifying they do not follow. Use your special skills," he said, giving Germaine a knowing look.

Nodding once, Germaine hopped off the porch and moved to the spot where Daniel had been prone on the ground. Squatting on his haunches, his fingers caressed the red needles. His scrutinizing gaze panned around him for a few moments, then, with a fast but decisive pace, he strode away in the direction Nolan and Daniel had come from earlier in the afternoon.

Nolan watched Germaine's figure become smaller, receding into the distance until he vanished into the landscape altogether. He sat down on a sawed-off section of tree stump next to Daniel. "Who's he?" he asked.

Daniel grinned. "He is much like you. At least when I found him eight years ago, he was much as you are now—full of energy yet confused about where to expend it. He thought himself all knowing, yet he continues to have a never-ending litany of questions," he said while winking at his young friend.

"He has a depth to him. Are you sure he wears a white hat?"

Pulling with both hands fixed on the arms of the chair, Daniel slid his butt forward. His back straightened, bringing his face close to Nolan's. "Germaine did not know of his psychic abilities eight years ago. At that time, I was employed to watch the Athar and investigate any abnormalities. Most days were quiet, but I sensed his ability and came to visit him often, just as we spend this time together now. Unfortunately, a Toltec watcher also saw the disturbance."

"Was it a rift because of a dream in the same way you found me?" the younger man interrupted.

"Indeed, it was. His dream was in the afternoon during what the people of your world calls a siesta, but that is immaterial." Daniel said, waving the thought away. "Sadly, the Toltec watcher killed Germaine's brother in an attempt to gain information as to his whereabouts." He sighed. "Germaine blamed me for a long time. Eventually, he learned that his path was linked to his destiny, and I was not integral to that process. Consequently, his anger toward me was redirected toward the Toltec—all of it. Since then, our friendship has grown." He lifted a finger to ensure Nolan's attention. "Do not get me wrong. I do not agree with all of his methods, but then we can't be right all the time. I remember when I went to school, if I was right 80 per cent of the time, people thought I was doing very well. Germaine easily makes the 80 per cent grade. He has a sense of honor with consideration of right and wrong driving his decisions, not greed or lust which are the basis of many people's goals. But then, who am I to judge?"

"You make it sound so simple."

"Life is only complicated because we make it so." Daniel was quick to respond.

Nolan couldn't hold back the chuckle. "See what I mean?"

"Enough then," Daniel countered as he rose to his now steady feet. "Let's get this place cleaned up."

For the next two hours the two men brought a semblance of order to the old wooden cabin. Daniel knew working on different tasks would be more efficient, but they worked side by side with both having the underlying sense their teamwork carried a higher consideration. They made short work of the exterior of the cabin, removing the boards from the three windows and two doors, and they only had to re-cover one pane of broken glass. Nolan found tools including a hammer and nails, allowing them to accomplish this task as well as stabilizing the loose deck boards with a few strategically placed fasteners. Once they entered the single room cabin, they were happy to see most things were not out of place. A thick layer of drab, gray dust covered every horizontal surface, complimenting the intricately engineered spider webs. The cleverly spun webs sparkled silver as the rays of the sun setting over the mountain fought through the patchy windows.

The windows and doors were opened wide, allowing the cool breeze to draft through the small structure. Finding brooms, they worked from the top down, clearing the dust and the webs to the displeasure of the spiders scurrying to the many crevices in the log walls. They frowned at the giants who brought turmoil to their peaceful world.

The dust not blown out by the breeze was swept from the outer walls toward the center of the room where a great stone fireplace stood. There are times where beauty is well described by a random pattern without rhyme or reason, and such was the case with the fireplace. It was open on two sides and comprised of rocks held together with mortar in an indiscriminate pattern of both size and color. The lower edge of the fireplace, where it met the stone floor, was eight feet across. The joined stones spiraled up six feet in height to a one-foot hole where it connected to a copper stack, and, from that point, it continued upward through the roof.

With the cleaning complete, the pair surveyed the contents of the room. There was a low couch with square cushions to one side of the fireplace and a single bed on the other. The mattress seemed acceptable for use, especially in comparison to the hard floor. With the additional mattress discovered in the storage closet, all three men would be off the floor at night.

There was an old oil stove on the small counter, in what loosely could be referred to as a kitchen, but with the limited fuel found, they decided the kerosene would be better used for the lamps in the room. The cooking could be done over the fireplace, as there was an abundant supply of dry stacked wood they had discovered against the east, outside wall.

With the cabin as clean as it had been for quite a few years, Nolan brought both their packs in from the porch, throwing his on the bed. "Where do you want your pack—the mattress or the couch?"

Bending his knee, Daniel crossed one foot over the other and leaned his hand against the fireplace, shrugging. "I am not overly particular, as I have slept in the best and worst of places."

The younger man sat on the bed, causing squeaks to escape from it as he bounced to test the coils.

"Germaine might not be happy though."

"What do you mean?" Nolan asked in mid-bounce.

"It's probably nothing," Daniel offered as he moved to the couch before pressing down with his hand, the motion barely budging the firm cushions.

"No really, what?"

"Germaine is from an unusual plane. They have very strict rules and they believe in—what do you call it here—a pecking order to things. Germaine does not know you at all, and I am sure he sees you as the new recruit—so to speak." He tilted his head and squinted, reflecting on his memory of Germaine. "Forget I mentioned it. He probably won't even notice."

Nolan relaxed his muscles.

"Assuming he is in his 80 per cent frame of mind."

Before Daniel's response was finished, Nolan had his butt on the old mattress set on the floor with his pack beside him. He glared at the older man who was making his way to the bed. Nolan opened his mouth for a smart-assed remark, but it was cut off by the double high-pitched notes sung by a bird in one of the trees close to the cabin.

Cupping his hand over his mouth, Daniel mirrored the sound back. "It's Germaine returning," he said as he rose and walked toward the cabin door.

The door creaked as it was pushed open on rusty hinges. The momentary look between Daniel and Germaine said much. In the fleeting instant, memories of the many battles they fought, side by side, showed through. Memories of the tears they shared due to the loss of ones they had loved, but above all, the trust they shared, was very evident. They both knew, in future battles and trepidations, they would both be there in the same manner—side by side. Nolan noticed the gaze with admiration and a hint of jealousy.

"What did you find?" Daniel asked as he secured the door behind Germaine.

"They followed the bait. I tracked back to the point where your path veered from theirs. North of the junction the path was heavily trodden. The

Kaezzarites were moving off in that direction with all haste, and I agree it would appear they number nine or ten strong," Germaine responded.

"So far, so good." Daniel smiled with a deep exhale. He was not sure until now if the ruse would really work.

As they moved over closer to the fireplace, Germaine continued. "I also set up perimeter warnings. If you hear the whistle of a chilo shell, it means someone has set off a wire."

"What is a chilo shell?" Nolan asked. He was always as curious as a puppy looking for something to chew on.

Turning toward the interruption, Germaine looked Nolan up and down before returning his gaze to Daniel. Seeing Nolan's slight nod, Germaine replied. "It's something from a plane called Drobinet. What's impressive is the coiled tunnel carved through the shell by the slug-like creature which thrives in the oceans of Drobinet. The sculls there discovered, long ago, if they drilled a small hole in the tip of the shell, and if air was blown through it, a shrill pitch amplified 20 times louder than you would imagine, considering the size of the shell, is emitted. As such, it's considered primarily a toy for children, but—" Germaine grinned mischievously "—when it's propped precariously in a tree it can be an effective alarm system. It just takes a thin piece of twine to be tied to a flexible branch of that tree, and if the twine is jostled by a languid foot, the acoustic pitch from the falling chilo will echo through these mountains and be heard from at least half a mile away."

Nolan listened to every word as Germaine reached into a long, previously indiscernible pocket running down from under his armpit for almost the length of his shirt. His fingers pulled out one of the chilo shells, holding its two-inch-high, conical shape covered in abalone like colors. Well described, the chilo shell was parked in Nolan's memory, and another question came to the forefront. "What's a scull?"

Daniel broke in with a response. "Scull is a slang term many purebloods use for all humans who have intermingled blood lines and, as a result, no psychic abilities. Centuries ago, it was a derogatory term since some pureblood races used sculls as slave labor. Today, in a more liberal Athar, it's just a name—a scull is a scull."

"As I've said before, you make things sound simple," Nolan muttered.

Daniel turned back to Germaine. "Do you have anything else to report?"

"Yes"

"What?"

"I'm famished. Don't you people eat on this planet?" Germaine asked.

The trio quickly set about preparations for dinner. Germaine brought in the wood, and in no time the unmatchable aroma of burning wood spread through the cabin, pushed on by the flames dancing around the fir logs. Nolan and Daniel, with their newly discovered teamwork, had a pot of mixed meat and pasta ready to place on the stone next to the fire, in no time. The marvel of convection brought the mixture to a boil in short order.

As hungry as Germaine was, he didn't outpace either of the other two men as they wolfed down their portions. The fine flavor of canned food increases inversely proportional to the length of time the stomach has been empty. As a result, the food they consumed tasted better than the finest five-star meal.

The sun had set some time ago, leaving the cabin dimly lit. The flickering shadows cast by the flames and the single lit lantern, bobbed up and down the rustic walls. The peaceful reprieve was welcomed by all three men, but especially by Nolan and Daniel, who had been on the run for the last two days. Such a reprieve, devoid of physical activity, transfers energy to the mind and gives people time to think, and when people think, they usually come up with more questions than answers.

"Okay, we're at the cabin." Nolan looked squarely at Daniel lazing on the couch. "What now?"

"We stay here—hopefully for three days to a week. You need to prepare for the biggest journey of your life," Daniel said.

Nolan shrugged. "I figured, from everything you've told me—and by the way, it wasn't easy to figure because everything you say is in riddles—well, I figured I wouldn't be safe until you train me to hop to one of your Celtae planes. That's the plan—right?"

The mention of Daniel's riddles caused Germaine to laugh.

Daniel lowered an eyebrow toward Germaine before returning his attention to Nolan and nodded. "My home world to be specific—Crann Bith."

"Do you think a fellow who has a few dreams about the stars and one unearthly dream of another plane, can suddenly hop from plane to plane in three days?" Nolan asked with his eyebrows raised incredulously.

"I said three days to a week," Daniel corrected. He looked in Nolan's eyes. "You lack confidence, and that is the worst thing that could happen. Come sit beside me."

Raising himself from his slouched position on the mattress, Nolan shifted to the more comfortable couch, next to the older man who cast an eerie shadow in the flickering light.

"I have told you a little of the Athar, and you have seen it, albeit in an uncontrolled process. Let me show you a little more of it. It will give you a hint of what is to come during your training," Daniel offered.

"Sure," Nolan replied. He kept his voice calm, but his body tensed in anticipation.

Daniel noticed Nolan's apprehension and said, "Let's talk about four things you need to understand to be able to navigate through the Athar. I have already mentioned the first thing you need, and that is *confidence*. You will need to truly believe each and every time you want to hop, that you can. The second thing is related to the first, and it is *relaxation*. You need to be in a relaxed frame of mind to hop planes. At times, it is difficult and requires much effort. Think on it. You might be running from an enemy in the heat of battle, yet your mind will need to be relaxed enough to allow the transposition."

The wide-eyed student listened to his mentor.

"The third thing you need to understand is *markers*. This is how we navigate the Athar. They are not so different from street signs on your world, giving definition to a point in space. The only difference is that you look at street signs with your eyes, and you will look at Athar markers with your mind."

A vibrating snore could be heard from Germaine who was laid out on Daniel's bed.

"There are also personal markers," Daniel continued. "You saw me use one in front of this cabin earlier today. The object you saw is made of a material that acts like a heat sink, only what it concentrates is psychic energy, not heat. It is draining, especially if one attempts to use it in a discrete manner. The three narrow banded pulses I sent were exactly that. So, when you see the Athar in your mind, you will see markers. It sounds complicated, but then, as an example, consider how many taxi drivers navigate their way around every street of New York City with or without the street signs. In a similar manner, traveling the Athar will become second nature to you."

Nolan's smile was limp with false confidence.

"The fourth and probably most important thing you need to know about is psychic wake," Daniel said.

"Wake—like a ship in water?"

"Exactly!" Daniel snapped his fingers. "Think of the Athar as being made of water. When a person hops planes, his energy moves through the Athar, leaving a wake. Two important things come to mind. One is the wake can be seen, and the second is things can be sucked into a wake. The wake from your peek into another plane during your dream was so large we have been calling it a rift, but it was really a wake. The characteristics of psychic wake are very important."

"What things can get sucked into a psychic wake?"

"Let me show you. I want you to focus, but, at the same time, try to stay relaxed." Daniel said.

Closing his eyes, Nolan tried to control his breathing, mimicking Lamaze techniques he had seen on an educational channel long ago.

"Now, focus, but let yourself relax. Blank out your mind, and you will see the markers," Daniel coaxed.

Nolan concentrated. He waited several seconds before words came to him. "I don't see any…" He jumped across the couch, almost falling over the wooden arm. "Freaking hell! What was that?" Nolan had felt Daniel's hand on his shoulder, and instantly, his mind's eye filled with bright, tightly-focused points of lights. Now, as he sat bug-eyed opposite Daniel, the view was gone. It was replaced with a view of Daniel's chiseled face, cut with a fatherly smile.

"Physical contact between purebloods channels one person's mind to the other person's wake. What you saw was fed by my mind's eye. Your mind went along for the ride, as it was sucked along my wake," Daniel explained much too nonchalantly for Nolan's liking.

"Bullshit!" Nolan blurted.

Another chuckle was heard from Germaine who was still prone on the bed.

"Don't mind him. He sleeps with one eye open," Daniel quipped. "Want to try again?"

Nolan's obsession to learn overcame his fear of the unknown, pulling him back next to the older man. Daniel placed his hand on Nolan's shoulder for a second time.

Closing his eyes and again relaxing his breaths, the foggy view of the Athar slowly sharpened. "I see it," Nolan managed with a shaky touch of amazement in his voice.

"Very good," Daniel said in an approving tone, much as a father would to a son after his first home run. "Now, I am going to take my hand off your shoulder. Let me know how long until the image fades away, okay?"

"Ready," Nolan replied. He felt the hand lift, and he tried to maintain the image, but it was only ten seconds before he said, "Gone."

"Not bad, really, Young Nolan, but we will practice this often for the next few days. The retention will be longer and longer until retention through my wake will be replaced solely by your own mind's eye. Now, let me show you one last thing," Daniel said as he put his hand on the younger man's shoulder for a third time.

Focusing as soon as he felt the pressure of Daniel's hand, the Athar came into view once more, but the event was noticeably faster than the previous instance.

"I want you to pick one of the markers and keep your mind's eye on it," Daniel directed.

"Okay—done."

"It's in the upper left quadrant of your view, correct?"

"Sure, but that isn't so hard. There's a 25 per cent probability of being right," Nolan said in an unimpressed tone."

"There are two markers in a vertical line directly to the right of your marker. The top one being, in fact, exactly in line with the marker you picked. There are three markers on a 45-degree angle below the marker in question. The top one in the line is just to the left of the subject marker. To the right of the…"

Nolan cut in. "I get it." Nolan opened his eyes and focused on Daniel. "That's freaking amazing."

"And there is so much more, but that will need to wait until tomorrow. Get your rest. You will need it," Daniel said with a finality that told Nolan, class was over.

As if on cue, Nolan yawned, stretching his arms up and behind him. "You don't need to convince me." He picked up one of the blankets they found in an upper cupboard and made his way past the fire, now reduced to embers. He dropped his weary frame onto the mattress.

Daniel took a few moments to finish the bottle of water he had been sipping from throughout the evening, then rose, making his way to Germaine sleeping on the bed. He slapped the slumbering figure hard on the side of the knee, uttering in a gruff voice, *"Aois a grinneas!"*

Eyes still closed, Germaine rose, shifting himself off the bed and onto the less comfortable couch. The soft snores returned almost before his head hit the cushion.

Lying on his back with his own eyes half closed, Nolan slurred, "What was that?"

Daniel slid onto the bed and crossed his feet. "Those were a few words from a language of long ago—from a time of honor and truth. You would not know the saying here, but it roughly translates to, *age before beauty.*"

Smiling as his eyelids closed out the firelight, Nolan thought—*that's freaking priceless.* The smile remained as sleep overtook him.

Chapter 12

Three sharp beeps resonated through the air of Julian's apartment.

He had been daydreaming while staring out the wall-to-wall glass windows covering the side of his three-room home. The beeps drew him from the corner he called a sunroom, up the three stairs, to the main living level and, finally, the kitchen. The beeps stopped when he unlatched the door to the oven. As invisible waves of heat hit his face, Julian scrunched his eyebrows and swore to himself. "Damn! Every time I heat food, I burn myself—*every* time." The ritual was completed the same way it was each time he felt his eyebrows singed. Looking at the pasta as if it was the root cause of the problem, he tossed the plastic container onto the counter top. The sound of the container spinning across the ceramic counter provided him with a level of comfort. Putting both hands on his hips, he waited for the wafts of steam to subside while his ears tuned into the sounds of the news report, live on the video monitor behind him in the main living area.

> *"It appears there were at least ten squads of Celtae strike soldiers involved in the raid on Kaezzar. What is becoming clear is a bomb was set off just yards from the Eye of the city, and the second bomb destroying Station 44 on the Industrial MagTrak line, were both diversions. Although there were 38 casualties at these two sites, we now know the primary target was the Bolivar Power Generating Station. State police stationed at the facility fought valiantly but were outmatched and quickly overrun by the Celtae elite forces which had appeared out of thin air. The death toll counted 24 heroes of the State, who gave their lives before military tactical reinforcements arrived on the scene."*

Now cooled sufficiently, Julian picked up the container of flavored pasta with the tips of his fingers. With his eyes glued to the three-foot-high by four-foot-wide monitor hanging on the far wall, his memory led his footsteps to his favorite spot on the black leather couch. As he filled his mouth with spoonfuls' of pasta, flashes of the battle at the power station filled the screen. The recorded film was shot by a newsperson using a high magnification drone camera hovering a mile from the hot point. As a result, it was fuzzy, but the red flashes of light were clearly the result of Toltec energy blasts making contact with Celtae energy shields. Figures could be seen running, and at this point in the confrontation, the Celtae were in retreat after destroying three of the 25 generators. Blue lines of laser fire crisscrossed the field of view, adding to the colorful night battle. Looking carefully amongst the patterns of light, Julian could see the rippled circles indicating the Celtae were hopping out after their devil's work was complete. *War is gruesome,* Julian thought, but then he corrected himself. *War is productive. It's actually the killing that's gruesome. It just happens to be an unfortunate by-product of war.*

As if on cue, the picture zoomed in on a hooded Celtae soldier with his figure rippling as his transposition cycle began. *It was unfortunate his face couldn't be seen,* Julian thought as a blue ray cut into the soldier's back. The focused ray diffused as it passed through his body. It then released from his chest in a wide, blue pattern mingled with chunks of flesh and organs. Julian squinted as the room lit up due to the video changing to a daytime shot. Overlaid in the upper right corner of the screen, in boxy letters, were the words – *LIVE FEED,* and the time – *1:35 p.m.* The scene showed the generating station with smoke still rising from the still red-hot metal in the background. The foreground was littered with several Celtae bodies that were turned and twisted in disturbing positions.

A female face popped up in the upper left corner. Julian thought she was pretty—too pretty to be doing commentary on gruesome war reports.

> *"And the attack was very costly to the Celtae. There have been 24 bodies counted, and it is expected more will be found once the generator station is safe to enter.*
>
> *It is not yet known what plane the terrorists came from, but Home State Security is investigating and promises a quick, decisive response once their origins are discovered.*
>
> *For the State Communication Network, this is Maria Tersa reporting."*

The video feed flipped back into the normally scheduled programming, providing a scene of small red lizards. They were the only creatures thriving on the arid salt flats covering most of this world. Naturalists would appreciate the lizard's position, but seeing the male on top of the female with his teeth holding her neck while he impregnated her, was repulsive to Julian.

Having finished the last spoonful of pasta, Julian made his way back to the picture window, observing the smoke from the power station far in the distance. *We were lucky,* he thought. Being the only power source for production of water and electricity to the city, it's the life and breath of Kaezzar. The power station—not only the power station—but the entire complex was an engineering marvel. Up on the third plateau some 50 miles away was a lake of lava. Just as the power station was an engineering marvel, Lake Fuego was just as fascinating a natural marvel. Almost perfectly round and 28 miles across, the lake was filled with bubbling, searing-hot lava. The lake was bottomless, and the lava tube narrowed as it corkscrewed down, providing the only heat vent from the planet's core. The marvel of nature was due to the balance of the system. Although there were some minor overflows from time to time, the lake kept the planet's temperature and the temperature of the world's core in balance. It was warmer near Lake Fuego and cooler as the distance increased from the heat source. Consequently, Kaezzar, without seasons, was always at a comfortably warm temperature.

How the early engineers of Kaezzar used Lake Fuego to their advantage still amazed Julian. Thousands of miles to the north, there was an ice pole. Winds, generated from the planet's rotation, over a very flat, arid planet, howled down at increasing speed. The winds were dry but not devoid of moisture. The high-speed winds would hit the cylinder of hot air in and around Lake Fuego, tumbling the cooler winds up and back over itself. The instantaneous pressure differential resulted in a torrential downpour over an 80-mile area just north of the molten lake.

With the absence of natural obstacles to block the supply of cold air, the cycle was repetitive. The torrential downpour was never ending, and as a result, Lake Fuente covered most of the upper northern plateau. With this never-ending supply of water, massive, breathtaking waterfalls dropped the flow to the second step of the plateau. The accelerating water continued downward, falling off the first step to the Great Plains where the flow evaporated quickly as the sun's balmy rays choked off the streams trying to form.

The abundance of potential energy was harnessed by the Engineering Corp. The waterfalls of the first step were sacrificed and replaced with a great dam housing 22 turbine generators, three of which were now destroyed in the attack. From the second level, two large river-like channels were cut into the stone plateau, controlling the flow of water down to the lower plains. A series of ten smaller generators lined each channel and supplemented the current from the main dam, but the system was still inefficient due to the fluctuations in water levels.

Herein lay the real engineering marvel. A twenty-mile-long tunnel was bored from Lake Fuente's upper reaches, skirting the edge of Lake Fuego.

As it flowed through, the water turned to steam and cranked the 25 steam generators in the insulated station close to the molten lake of lava. Not only did this provide additional electricity, but the flow could be controlled, stabilizing the flow of water through the dam.

Julian surveyed the east side of the city containing most of the industrial sector. It was common sense for the factories to be located there, as the large overland water pipes and the high voltage power lines suspended from towers, entered the city from that side.

Lowering himself onto a stool on the tiled floor, he reached into his jacket pocket, pulling out the picture. Tracing his fingers over the face surrounded by blonde hair and highlighted by a rugged moustache, Julian mumbled, "Who are you? With all the marvels of technology around us, do you think someone could tell me who you are?" When Sub-Commander Rankin brought him the picture first thing this morning, he scanned it and entered it into the security database, but nothing matched. That wasn't surprising considering the limitations of such a repository in the infinite nature of the Athar. He would need some clues to narrow down the search.

Tapping his index finger on the picture, he talked to the cold, blue eyes. "Don't get me wrong. I don't give up so easily, so I'll find you out. The incompetent fools of Red Squad still have come up with nothing, but even they will not cause me to lose my resolve." A callous smile crossed his lips. "After all, don't forget. You and your friend are my ticket up the ladder. I just know it."

Chapter 13

Half-Ear lay on the cool soil amidst the tall grass and looked down from the high ground with his snout resting across his wide paws. Even though his body was old and bent, his amber eyes were still sharp, spying down on the tall-leg's den.

Half-Ear had made the tall-leg's den his own over the cold after he left his wolf brothers and sisters. He had been the lead for three cycles of cold to warm, but as it is in all packs, young blood will challenge, and the old must move on to travel on their own. The fight for lead had not been without injury, leaving his left foreleg ripped open by sharp claws. Unable to hunt, the tall-legs shelter and the frozen white-tail hanging from the roof of the den, were the only things saving him from the cold death of the mountains.

With the snow melting and the white-tail nothing but bone, Half-Ear needed to eat, and to eat he needed to hunt, so he tested the leg. The test proved he would never have the speed to catch even a baby hoof-kicker or a white-tail, but the leg held him well enough so he caught long-ears, small-furs and even some slimy-hoppers. The nourishment allowed him to regain his strength while the coming warmth turned buds to leaves on the protective trees.

Two suns ago, he had left his borrowed den to hunt, and now, on his return, his nose lifted, smelling the unmistakable fire-smoke which came with the tall-legs when they brought their thunder-death. But death no longer worried Half-Ear. He knew this would be his last warm season. His body, although stronger, ached—the type of ache deep within his bones, which he knew would become worse and leave him for frozen-dead over the next cold. It was not a good death. He often considered if he should jump off a cliff to end his life, his bones cracking on the rocks and tree limbs as Black-Paw before him had done.

For now, the tall-legs piqued his interest, so Half-Ear did not run or jump. Rather, he stayed, and his mind moved to more pleasurable thoughts. As the morning sun rose over the trees, it warmed his back, signaling him to turn and let the heat caress his belly. If someone could read a wolf's mind, they would see Half-Ear, with his impending fatality freeing him of apprehension, looking forward to the challenge of the tall-legs, and if there was such a thing as a wolf's smile, this is what they would see covering his pointed face.

Nolan felt the warmth of the sun on his face as the bright morning rays spilled through the patchy windows on the west side of the cabin. He was in a lucid state, half asleep with the tranquility keeping his mind from fully awakening to the turmoil of the day. His mind told him to keep his eyes closed and return to the peace of his dreams, but voices barely above a whisper kept him on the edge of awareness.

"Are you sure?" Germaine whispered.

Daniel's voice, even more subdued, responded. "Nothing is for certain, my friend. I have told you what I know. The science says the rest."

"If indeed the *First Key* has been found, as prophesized, it will bring turmoil to our Athar."

"Only for a time," Daniel whispered. "If we are committed and follow through as we have always vowed, the turmoil could well be replaced by a lasting peace. It is the goal we have fought and many others have died for."

"But this is only the start. The Second and Third Keys are needed to complete the prophesy, so the purebloods can be convinced peace is an option," Germaine offered.

Nolan shifted as his mind took him in and out of his dream state. One second, he was in his subconscious, the next, he barely heard the whispers before his mind coaxed him back into sleep. His dream mixed with the pieces of sentences he heard, merging into a jumble of thoughts stored deep in the recesses of his brain.

Hearing him shift, Daniel looked over at Nolan. Once he heard the deep breaths of sleep return, Daniel turned his gaze back to Germaine. "There is a long road ahead of us, but the road of war forever killing our people is even longer."

Leaning forward, Germaine whispered, "He's young. Are you sure he can handle what comes with being the First Key?"

"I told you nothing is for certain." An edge of irritation entered Daniel's voice. "But I am committed, and as such, will train him so he is at least prepared for what is to come. The rest will be up to him."

Hearing the irritation, Germaine reaffirmed his position. "Daniel, we are more than friends. I'm committed to the cause, but even more so, I'm committed to you." He held his hand out.

Daniel closed his fingers around Germaine's forearm and, at the same time, felt Germaine's strong fingers grasp his own. "I could ask for nothing more, my friend. Best you be off, then. Check the perimeter, and keep your eyes open for trouble."

Without a word, Germaine rose and slid out the door with the frame hitting the door jamb, hard, behind him. The clang of the door, followed by the rattle of the old knob, finally brought Nolan from the dream world, with his energy refreshed for the day ahead.

Half-Ear rolled and rolled in the dust bath. He had found the soft dirt hidden on the far side of three large rocks after the snow melt. It was all that was left of the place where the tiny, red eight-legs lived. He had waited until he was sure that all the itchy things were gone before he flattened the mound, and since then, he had used it many times for his pleasure. Hearing the crack of wood on wood he twisted to his feet as his ears lifted high. His tuned ears heard the footsteps of a tall-leg just down the mountainside. Shaking his body, front quarter twisting in the opposite direction to his rear quarter, the dust suspended in a fog around the old wolf. With a tilt of his head, silent footfalls took him to the rocky outcrop where he knew he would be able to see down to the tall-leg's den.

As Half-Ear's proud face looked over the large rock, he saw the long-hair tall-leg disappear into the forest, carrying two shiny sticks. He blew the dust out of his nose. There were tall-legs who lived where the sun rose over the big water. They used the same type of shiny sticks to open white-tails and big-hoofs before they would eat them. The shiny sticks were *danger*, but no more danger than his sharp bite.

Half-Ear lay down on the rock, peering over the edge, waiting for the other two tall-legs to come out of the den. In the last sun, the old tall-leg amused Half-Ear with the bright lightning which came from his hands. He would watch with even more interest today. He heard the crack of wood on wood once again, and without taking his belly off the rock, he shimmied himself forward to get a better view of the two tall-legs who were on the flat wood in front of the den. These two did not have the shiny sticks nor did they have the thunder-sticks which brought death to all. Half-Ear cocked his head. Too bad. Fighting a tall-leg with a thunder stick would be a good death—better than lying huddled in a cave while waiting for the cold to take him back to the dust of the Earth.

He watched the pair sit on the small wooden ledges, bringing their legs under them as only tall-legs could do. They touched each other and made sounds only tall-legs could understand. Half-Ear recognized the signals. The old one was teaching the tall-leg pup, just as Black-Paw taught him many seasons ago. Half-Ear realized the old one was leader of their pack, but he watched the pup with curiosity. The tall-leg pup looked the old one straight in the eye and kept his shoulders square to him. Half-Ear knew, one day, the pup would lead.

Nolan sat on the tree stump, holding the container of orange juice. He brought the thin straw to his lips, sucking until the gurgle indicated the vessel was empty. He looked at the green fir trees and listened to the birds singing in their midst, knowing this was but a respite. Perhaps it was his psychic abilities showing through and somehow telling him blood and death would soon cloud the serene image.

Daniel interrupted Nolan's daydream. "It's time to begin."

"Show me how to invoke the energy shield."

Daniel lifted his hat, fingers of one hand at the front, fingers of the other hand holding the brim at the back, and with a gentle tug, the old leather hat was settled into place on his head. "That is one of the last things I will teach you. First, you must learn to touch the Athar, and from there, you will learn how to navigate it. If things go as expected, in a few short days, hopefully, we will hop away from the danger pursuing you in this forest."

"How do I touch the Athar?" Nolan queried.

"With confidence and concentration in a relaxed state."

"What the freaking hell does that mean?" the younger man asked.

"You will need to be like a spider."

Nolan frowned. "You're losing me even before we begin."

Daniel leaned forward. "You will need to be able to focus part of your mind on the Athar even though other events distract and occupy your thoughts." The older man's finger straightened, pointing to the large spider web, the intricate pattern filling the corner where the roof met the wall under the eave. "Do you see the spider?"

Peering into the shadows, Nolan finally saw the spider playing across the web with its small head connected to a massive torso ending in a curled point. "I see it," he said.

"It looks like he has just caught a wasp. Do you see him wrapping the unfortunate meal in its silk?"

Nolan sighed. "Of course, but what does this have to do with the Athar?"

"If you want to learn, Young Nolan, then please provide less talking and more listening," Daniel chastised. He reached down, picking up the long, thin twig lying under his chair. Raising it, he lightly flicked the closest corner of the spider web. "Watch."

Stopping immediately, the spider came over to the area still vibrating from the impact of the twig. Once it determined nothing was caught in the sticky tendrils, it scooted back into the heart of the web, with its efforts again focused on the tight wrap it was placing around the wasp. Daniel flicked the spider web again, and again the eight-legged arachnid danced over along its silken ladder to investigate. Once again, after seeing nothing was there, it went quickly back to the wasp. For a third time Daniel flicked the web with the tip of the twig. The spider's legs stopped for an instant, but did not move from the wasp. On the fourth flick the spider did not pay any attention to the vibration at all.

"What did you see?" Daniel posed the question to Nolan.

"Nothing I can think has any connection in any way, shape or form to the Athar," Nolan retorted.

Chuckling, Daniel sat back. "The spider was a quick study. In a short time, it learned to keep its focus on the wasp even though another part of the web was being disturbed. Do you think you will learn as quickly to keep your focus on the Athar while others are beating their sticks along your path?"

Nolan did not answer, preferring to glare at his mentor.

"Concentration with relaxation and confidence will prove you superior to the spider. The keys to those attributes will be a clear mind, physical fitness and breathing technique." Daniel tapped Nolan's chest with the tip of the twig. "*You* need to be in control."

Four hours later, Nolan felt like he was anything but in control. Rather, frustration and weariness were foremost in his mind. There was a distinct pattern to Daniel's training. They would spend quite some time reaching the Athar in the same manner accomplished the night before, when Nolan had looked along Daniel's psychic wake. Each time Daniel took his hand off Nolan's shoulder, the Athar would vanish. To Nolan's surprise, he realized the image of the Athar in his mind's eye remained for longer and longer each time it was invoked, but each time, just as Nolan was feeling as if he was making some headway, Daniel would order him up. The older man would then lead Nolan in a run through the woods around the cabin over a distance of approximately 200 yards. When Nolan arrived back at the porch of the cabin, panting for breath, Daniel would move him through a string of calisthenics. There was a series of push-ups, sit-ups and leg exercises, taxing Nolan's muscles and lungs to the bursting point.

Once those were done, the mentor would direct his student in breathing exercises to bring him quickly back to a relaxed state. A quick deep breath in—a four second hold—followed by a two second exhale while pressing his palms on his thighs. If Nolan's technique was remiss, Daniel would snap him with the twig he retained throughout the training, specifically for that purpose. The cycle was repeated over and over—the Athar wake—the physical exercise, then the breathing. Nolan was exhausted, but as the sun began to creep well past the zenith, he could hold the vision of the Athar for three minutes. He was excited but also hungry.

"How about a late lunch?" Nolan asked through pants as they ran their course around the cabin.

"Sounds good," Daniel answered. "We have some more canned meat and pasta."

They made the final uphill turn back to the cabin. "No canned food for me." Grinning as he arrived at the porch, Nolan asked, "I want some fresh food. Do you like fish?"

"Of course, but you have no means to catch a fish," Daniel said as he leaned his teaching twig against the cabin's outside wall.

Nolan pushed a finger into Daniel's chest, a wide smile forming on his face. "Now there you're wrong, my friend." He raced into the cabin, searching through his pack and found the mini-rod with the telescoping shaft, he stored at the last minute before leaving the Neilton hardware store. He rushed out just as quickly, showing Daniel the rod as proudly as if it was his first-born cradled in his arms.

"Well done!" Daniel laughed. "You have the rod. Now all you need is the water and from such a combination, hopefully, a fish."

"You forget I know these mountains very well. There's a stream just south of here, so follow along," Nolan proudly replied.

"Are you sure?"

Quick as a fox, Nolan picked up Daniel's twig, slapping the older man in the chest with it. "Less talking and more listening. You might learn something." Nolan mimicked the older man's raspy voice before turning off in a run toward the stream he knew lay south of the cabin.

Nolan sliced through the fir trees, avoiding the rocks freckling the open grass, and all the while he heard the older man close on his heels. Suddenly, both Nolan's heels dug in, bringing him to an almost instant stop not 20 yards from the large timber wolf. It sat passively blocking their path to the stream.

Daniel's reaction time was not as good, and his chest crashed into Nolan's back, sending them both pitched forward onto their bellies in the tall grass.

"Let me handle this," Daniel whispered. "I will use the energy shield to protect us if need be."

"No, he poses no danger," Nolan said. He didn't take his eyes off the tall timber wolf whose gray fur was streaked with thin lines of brown. "If he was aggressive, he would have attacked when we fell. Besides, he is good luck."

"I have not seen a wolf in a long time. He is old and does not look so lucky."

Nolan kept his voice low. "He has some years on him, but don't be fooled. His stomach is thin, but his shoulders are wide and well-muscled. The natives who once roamed these forests, but now live on the reservation along the coast, hold the wolves as sacred creatures. Almost always, these wolves are seen in packs. A lone, older wolf, such as we are seeing here, is very rare. To the natives, such a sighting is seen as a foretelling of good luck, so we don't want to aggravate him and ruin the omen. Rise slowly and walk to your right so as not to disturb him. Follow my lead."

Daniel nodded his head and followed the younger man's direction, taking careful footsteps into the forest on their right. As Nolan shimmied to his right, he looked into the wolf's face seeing half of his left ear missing. *It probably occurred in a territorial fight,* he surmised. Next, his gaze moved down to the wolf's eyes. He knew better than to appear aggressive, but he knew just as well that it would be their undoing if he showed fear.

Half-Ear was surprised. The tall-legs did not run, and they did not show fear. They gave him his space, and this was unusual for tall-legs, but then these tall-legs did many strange things. Half-Ear had watched from the rock above their den for most of the day. He was no longer sure if the old tall-leg was teaching or if they were playing. They sat—then they ran, then they sat again. These tall-legs seemed stupid, as they ran and ran, but after all their effort, they found themselves in the spot where they began. He knew if these two were wolves, they would have been cast out of the pack long ago.

The tall-leg pup has good eyes. Half-Ear looked into the gray eyes and saw spirit matching his own. These tall-legs seemed different to those he had seen bring death. Perhaps he just missed his pack. Perhaps he had become soft in his loneliness. The thought left his mind as quickly as it came. He pushed up on his front legs, bounding along a parallel path to the one the tall-legs walked on their way to the running water.

Daniel kept his ears alert. "The wolf is following."

"He is curious more than anything else," Nolan said. "I don't think we need to worry about him."

The sound of the thin layer of water sliding along the pebbly stream bottom told the men they were close to the stream. Within minutes they passed a final thicket of tall brush, and the stream came to life before them. The water was two feet at its deepest point, churning and spraying as it made a slow curve from their position until it disappeared around a crag of rocks in the distance.

Nolan leaned over, surveying the pebbly shoreline as he mumbled over and over, "We need bait—we need bait."

The older man crossed his arms and waited, watching Nolan as his search took him further back into the thicket. When he heard Nolan whoop in triumph, he sauntered over to join the younger man, where he found him on his knees with his fingers sifting through an animal stool.

With his face contorting with disgust, Daniel said, "You have your fingers in feces."

"You're mistaken. Feces are what a nurse collects in a hospital bed pan. This is the wild, and this is shit—bear shit by the smell of it."

Daniel was speechless with his mouth hanging open.

"Since bear shit is high fiber, it's also a good place to find grubs." Nolan lifted his fingers out of the dried shit, holding up two of the curly, white grubs. "These will do well enough for fish bait."

"But it was living in the…"

"…the shit—I know. The fish like them just fine," Nolan said as he put the grub on the hook while walking back to the stream.

Daniel took off his hat and scratched his head. "Let me understand. The grub was in the shit. The fish will eat the grub—and you expect me to eat the fish?"

Pulling his arm back, Nolan cast the hook holding the impaled grub into the water. Almost weightless, it floated with the strong current, but it vibrated as Nolan gave it small tugs. *It's a poor man's fly rod,* he thought. Keeping his eyes on the grub he asked Daniel, "Do you like mushrooms?"

"On this world, I have eaten them more than a few times, preferring them in a red wine sauce. Unfortunately, they do not grow on my home world," the older man answered while his eyebrow rose, showing his curiosity about the question.

"It might taste good in a wine sauce, but they grow them in shit—pig shit being the most effective. Mushrooms are the same as the fungus you've seen growing on the rot in the fallen trees." He turned his eyes to Daniel and said casually, "Rot—just another word for shit. The same bacteria live in both."

Daniel's jaw dropped.

"Do you like a good steak?" Nolan continued the assault on Daniel's palate. He reeled in the line and caste the grub out again, but further this time.

"I like a medium-rare steak."

"Well, a steak is from a cow no matter how you cook it. Cows eat grass, and the grass is full of fertilizer," Nolan said, his tone even more casual. "Fertilizer is just another word for shit. You see, in the end, all things come from shit." He shook his head. "I'm not going to even *start* to tell you where eggs come from."

Daniel lost all his color. The graphic of the egg's origin played in his mind, and he could not clear it until he saw Nolan's fishing line go taut. Nolan reacted and pulled, causing the telescoped rod to bend under the strain. It took him several minutes to bring in the salmon. Once reeled in, he saw it was 16 inches of fight that would soon be in a frying pan. He hooked a string through a gill and tossed the fish over his shoulder. "You might feel different about the fish after you smell it cooking." He winked at the older man as he started back to the cabin.

The tall-legs caught a swimmer! Half-Ear watched the tall-leg pup carry it back to their den. He ate a swimmer only once, finding the half-eaten flesh left on the shoreline of a river. It was all that was left after the giant-paw filled its belly. The meat tasted different, almost like the slimy hoppers living in the forest ponds. He finished the swimmer just before the giant-paw came back. The roar from the giant-paw's mouth had warned Half-Ear, but not before the large hooked claws nicked his hind quarter. Since then, he ran on the paths the giant-paws did not travel.

The sight of the swimmer made Half-Ear hungry, and his belly rumbled in response. He was no longer quick enough to catch a swimmer, but he knew a spot where the long-ears ate the grass under thick branches that kept the flying-claws away. He opened his mouth while his long tongue wrapped around his thin lips as he padded off in a sideways trot to his forecasted meal.

The frying pan still held a few morsels of salmon lying in the thin layer of cooking oil. Germaine, having returned as the sun set over the mountain, joined Daniel and Nolan in consuming the fresh catch.

The lateness of the day turned lunch into dinner. As Nolan expected, the aroma of the fresh fish filling the small cabin made the older man hungry. As the meat sizzled and popped in the pan sitting at the edge of the burning fire, any reservations Daniel had about the grub was easily overcome. He devoured his share and more. Apparently, Germaine also found a new level of respect for the younger Earthman, now that his belly was full, and, at least temporarily, biased his opinion.

There were times when joviality, laughter and intelligent discussion were the activities friends shared. This was not one of those times. With the sweet taste of the fish still on their lips, and their bodies tired from the day's activities, the stillness of the cabin, interrupted only by distant night animals sounds, made the perfect setting for their silent camaraderie. The tranquil mood lasted for over an hour before Nolan arose, picking up the plates and the frying pan, before transporting them to the sink along the far wall. Nonchalantly, he reached for the pail with the remains of the fish carcass. The head and tail still had a sufficient amount of meat attached to them, so he tipped them over the cooked scraps in the frying pan. Considering the size of the fish, the pan was overflowing. Consequently, he took careful steps as he made a path to the front door of the cabin.

"The wolf is a wild animal," Daniel said, tilting his head back while watching Nolan with the fish pile. "You saw its eyes. It is perhaps not so smart, but it is a proud animal and will starve before it takes a handout from a human."

"I guess we'll find out, won't we." Nolan retorted.

"You're just wasting your energy," the mentor replied. His head turning toward the fire was a cue indicating the topic was finished.

Nolan held his hand on the door knob, paused, then turned to face the older man. "It's wasting your *time*, not wasting your energy."

"What?" Daniel said as he turned his face back toward Nolan.

Curious about the statement, Germaine also lifted his eyes to the young man.

"This is Earth. We don't waste our energy. The saying here is— 'Don't waste your time.'" He held his finger and thumb together in a circle with his chin jutting out to emphasize his point.

Daniel was miffed, his eyebrows slanted, showing his confusion. "That's ridiculous. Time is a constant at any place in the Athar. It can neither be wasted nor accumulated. Energy is the correct term. I repeat, you are wasting your energy." His finger pointed toward the frying pan.

Nolan raised his head, laughing. "Very well then, my teacher. It's wasting energy if you wish, but I'll still leave the scraps outside the door for the wolf." With that, he turned, opened the creaky door and placed the pan just outside on the wood stump he was accustomed to sitting on.

Looking at Germaine, Daniel said "Nolan did well today. It was much better than you did on your first day."

Germaine chortled, "Ha," then sat forward on the couch. "It's just as well that he best be able to travel soon. So far there are no sign of the Kaezzarites, but they'll be here soon. I can smell it."

"I'm not ready," Nolan interrupted. "I can barely hold the vision of the Athar in my mind. If I ever learn to hop, it'll not be for some time."

"Don't underestimate what you have accomplished today. You made great progress. Very soon, you *will* be ready to make a hop," Daniel reassured the younger man. "Come here. I have something to help you."

Nolan watched Daniel with curious eyes as the older man reached into his shirt pocket. The older man removed a small pouch of wax paper, and in it were several small, red pills. "Now that you have some training, you could access the Athar again, and that would be unfortunate, considering your control is limited. The Kaezzarites would be on us in an instant if you created another large rift. These pills keep your mind on a middle ground, taking out the highs and lows. It will help your training, but it will also keep your mind from trampling through the Athar for all to see." He gave the packet to Nolan. Take one pill now and the others at 12-hour intervals."

Taking the pouch, Nolan popped one pill in his mouth while the others were placed in his shirt pocket for safekeeping. "It's at times like this I feel so helpless, and this leads to my frustration. There seems so much I still need to learn."

"My psychic ability tells me there is a line of questions coming." Daniel winked at Nolan.

Ignoring the older man's amusement, Nolan asked, "You say I'm a pureblood, and it would seem so from the way I can see in your wake, but why me? Why does this insignificant man—" He pointed a finger at his heart "—have these special powers here on Earth?"

Daniel's voice was filled with sincerity. "You are not insignificant." He shook his head from side to side. "You have great potential, and you could be a key to the direction of the war and the resulting future of the Athar. You were obviously a special child. Nature, every so often, under the right circumstances, creates a rare genetic combination. In some ways, you are no different than a very tall man. The average human is what—five-foot-eleven-inches tall? But there is the very rare human who surpasses seven feet tall. You follow the same pattern except your gift is mental, not physical."

Nolan did a double take when the word *key* nudged an entrenched memory deep in his mind. It faded quickly, replaced by a sudden revelation. His eyes narrowed at Daniel as he rose to his feet, hovering above him. "How do you know I am a Celtae? I could be Toltec, Anasazi or any one of the other four races you say are extinct."

Daniel and Germaine exchanged nervous glances before the older man responded. "I know you are Celtae because the first night, while you slept under the stars, I took a blood sample and analyzed it. That night the water you drank had a mild drug in it so you would not awaken."

Nolan could feel his teeth grinding under clenched lips, and he instinctively bent his arm up. His opposite hand moved to the crook at his elbow as he remembered the ache. His eyes bored into the older man. Barely above a whisper, he said, "Do you know what a *mulligan* is?"

Germaine was surprised to see the look of dejection in Daniel's eyes as he heard him respond, "No."

"There's a popular game here on earth called golf. Between friends there is a rule, whereby if one player completely misses a shot, he can replay the shot without a penalty. It is available only once during the game."

Germaine saw confusion added to Daniel's dejected look.

Nolan's eyes didn't leave the older man. "In this game *you* are playing, you just used your mulligan. Don't you *ever* get in my space again."

The boy has spirit, Daniel thought. He will be a leader one day, and others will follow him. "My apologies. I had my reasons, but they are not excuses. Let's keep our trust. It won't happen again."

With that indiscretion considered closed, Nolan moved toward his mattress and sat on the edge with his mind still going a mile a minute. He was still angry, but he forced a crack of a smile to his lips. "I suppose we are even today."

"What do you mean?" Daniel replied.

"We both have learned something today. I learned you violated my space, and I taught you the finer points of eating shit." That said, Nolan stretched out, covering himself with the blanket.

Daniel was not sure what to say, but thankfully, Germaine's boisterous guffaws broke the tension, and then all three men were laughing together. As Daniel and Germaine also made ready for sleep, the laughter faded, replaced by serene quiet. At least it was so in the cabin surrounded by nature's night sounds.

Nolan's mind was altogether a contrast. His head still whirled. He was a Celtae! He had the power of the shield! There was so much he learned, and there was even more to learn tomorrow. Perhaps tomorrow the shield would flare into life around his body.

His heart was pumping with a quickened pace. He needed sleep, but first he needed to slow his mind, so he invoked the breathing exercises he learned earlier in the day. One deep inhale—hold and then a long exhale. In a short time, he was relaxed with his breaths coming slow and deep. His eyes were closed with his mind on the edge of the subconscious, when it trickled in front of his mind's eye. It was very dim at first, but then it became clearer and clearer. The vision of the Athar was bright in his mind. As it is in the space between the dream world and reality, not all things made sense. In the morning, when he awoke, his conscious mind might not remember Daniel's hand was not on his shoulder, and that this vision was brought to life solely by his own mind.

Chapter 14

It normally took between two to four seconds for a pureblood to hop from one plane to another. During that time, the person's body is in a state close to non-existence, not really having left the origin plane yet not fully in the plane being traveled to. There are no thoughts, dreams or conscious brain activities of any type during this time span.

Julian had hopped many times, enjoying the thrill of the ride. The feeling was unmatchable. It began with a sense of falling to then being suddenly wrenched upright by invisible hands. The vertigo feeling along with the butterflies in the stomach, felt like it came and went at the same instant. When the feeling subsided and he opened his eyes, he knew he would be at his destination.

As the ripples around his body faded and his molecules solidified, Julian viewed Red Squad parked against a thicket of trees providing shelter from the early morning droplets of rain. He looked skyward where the soft raindrops were such a contrast to the pounding pelts of water which fell on the Upper Plateau above his home city of Kaezzar. Turning his head, he saw Sub-Commander Rankin had materialized beside him, as planned, and he thought, *her face looks gaunt.* She had substantial hop experience, but that's not the same as hopping into a field situation like the one presenting itself in front of them at this moment.

"Everything okay, Rankin?" Julian probed.

Without looking back at Julian, she replied, "Just fine, Commander. I've not seen such a soft rain before." She held her hand out, palm up, letting the tiny droplets land and roll off her fingers.

"You might learn a few new things today, Sub-Commander," Julian replied in a coy tone.

Captain Enriquez walked across the short field of intermingled grass and rock to their position. "Welcome to Earth," he said as his hand skipped across his brow in a motion somewhere between a salute and a wave.

Julian scrutinized the man. He was tall for a Toltec at six-foot-two-inches. His beard and moustache, sodden with moisture, had become scraggly, and his brown eyes were weary.

As he pulled on a pair of thin, black leather gloves, Julian said, "Thank you, Captain. I understand you've finally caught up with the five people you've been following, but to my chagrin, I've been told the five has somehow reduced to three."

"Our intelligence was incorrect," Enriquez said apologetically.

Julian didn't move to the cover of the trees. He saw Enriquez was already water-logged, and Rankin was beginning to fidget in her discomfort with the dampness. "But it was the runners from *your* squad who told me there were five people in this group, including Nolan Harrison and his mysterious partner known only as Daniel." The commander pressed home his point.

"That was in fact the report, but it's now obvious the report of five was flawed."

"Do you mean to tell me Red Squad, the elite of Watch Command, heralded across the Athar, were duped by a scull and an old man!" Julian's voice rose as he tore into Captain Enriquez.

The captain ignored the insult. "We've questioned the three captives at length. They have not seen the pair we search for since the morning they left the town of Neilton, three days ago."

"Did they have anything else to say?" Julian probed.

"They know nothing else."

"Give me your pistol, Captain."

Enriquez's eyes blinked nervously for a few seconds. "My pistol?"

"Yes, your pistol. I'm going to give Sub-Commander Rankin a lesson in the relationship between field probability and scull group psychology," Julian replied with an amused look on his face.

Captain Enriquez undid the clip on his holster, slid the energy pistol out and placed it in Julian's out-turned hand.

The commander turned his back on the captain, a sure sign he was dismissed. Facing Rankin, he toyed with the gun, checking the safety and the small pins on the side that set the intensity and disbursement of the beam. "You took psychology in the Academy, correct?"

"Yes," Rankin replied as water rolled in small drips from her nose.

"Including typical interrogation methods?" Julian asked.

"Standard curriculum, Sir."

"Then, let's see what you recall. If you have one prisoner, what is the probability of him telling you what you want to know?" Julian questioned.

"Depends."

"On what, Sub-Commander?" Julian continued the line of questions.

"Fear."

Julian placed the gun in his belt, muzzle down. "Very good. So, look at the scene over there." Julian pointed to the location where the three hikers were kneeling under a tree. "Evaluate the setting and tell me the probability of one man telling me what I need to know."

Rankin squinted, peering through the rain. The two soldiers who were guarding the prisoners were very relaxed with their guns slung over their shoulder, and one was smoking tobacco. The other men of Red Squad were talking jovially under the protection of a wide-spread maple, leaving the last two men on guard at each end of their perimeter. "The guards are relaxed. It would make sense to think the prisoners are also relaxed. Odds are very low you would learn anything—perhaps ten per cent."

"Agreed," Julian said as he rubbed his chin. "But there are three prisoners. What does that do to the odds?"

"It lowers it to almost nothing. Particularly with men, there is a bravado that would give them unity. Consequently, it's unlikely they would say anything for fear of looking weak in front of the others."

Julian chuckled. "So, fear is the key again. Let's get fear back on our side. Suppose we injure one of them?" Julian offered with one eyebrow raised quizzically.

Sub-Commander Rankin's stare became ice cold. "Obviously the odds would swing toward the truth coming out. I would say an injury would result in at least a 70 per cent probability they would tell the truth. It would be quite a bit higher for the injured man and a little lower for the other two who watched."

"Correct again! And that's what they teach you in the Academy from their text books, but there are no books here, are there?" Without waiting for a response, Julian left Rankin and walked briskly toward the three prisoners, pulling the gun from his belt. He faced squarely toward the big man with the red hair—the one called Jeffrey Larmer. "Where is this man?" he asked, pointing to the blonde figure in the picture he had pulled from his pocket.

"We already told your friends we don't know…"

Big Red's mouth was gapped open, and his eyes were wide with surprise. With a flick of his wrist, Julian had aimed at the center of the big man's forehead, then tugged on the hairpin trigger. The thin, blue ray sizzled into the front of the hiker's head. He was dead before the burst exited out the back side.

Julian turned to the two surviving men before Big Red's body had time to hit the ground and said, "I hate negativity." Just as abruptly, he turned and walked back toward Rankin.

The joviality of Red Squad stopped as they heard the energy burst. To a man, their jaws were slack in shock at the callousness from one of their own. Rankin, just as shocked, was white as a ghost, looking through Julian toward the dead man whose latent nerve impulses caused his leg to spasm.

"Now, here is what they do *not* teach you in the Academy!" With wild eyes, Julian said, "Some might think, since there are only two prisoners left, I have reduced my odds, but the two who are left are so scared they have a whole new definition of 'scared!' What are the odds I will get the truth?"

Rankin opened her mouth to speak.

Julian interrupted. "Exactly—about 90 per cent! In a rather perverse twist on fear, those two are brothers." Julian laughed. "So, they're not as afraid of dying as they are afraid to see the other die. In my book that's worth another five per cent, bringing our probability of hearing the truth to at least 95 per cent!"

Rankin just nodded her head up and down.

"The more they think about it, the higher our probability goes. As a result, by the time I walk back over there, I'll have a 100 per cent certainty they'll tell me absolutely everything they know." He paused, giving Rankin a sinister look. His words now came slowly. "They don't teach you *that* in a text book."

Turning on his toe, Julian strut his small frame back over to the two brothers, not caring if Rankin followed. Once in front of the two trembling men, he asked. "Who can tell me about Daniel?"

Both of the brothers began blithering at the same time, talking over each other.

"Wait—wait!" Julian yelled. "You first." He pointed to the man on his left.

Nick Milton took a deep breath. "He was in the town restaurant when we came into Nielton a few nights ago. We had a little too much to drink, and we got into an altercation."

Robert Milton cut in. "After that, we didn't see them until the next morning at breakfast. At least we saw Daniel the next morning. His friend Nolan was still sleeping."

"When people have breakfast, they talk. What did he say? Think carefully now," Julian said as he fingered the gun.

Nick was the first to speak. "It was a pretty quiet breakfast. Daniel had lain a lickin on Jeff the previous night." His eyes turned momentarily to look at the corpse beside him, choking on the words. "So, there wasn't a lot said. We asked where they were going, but he didn't say too much. He just said it was a long journey, and this was just the first step."

Robert jumped into the conversation. "Red Sea."

"Red Sea?" Julian echoed.

With fear in his eyes, Robert looked up at Julian. "I remember it was a bright morning. We talked casually about it, but Daniel said, at his home, he saw a lot of haze. He called it a 'Red Sea.'" Robert shrugged. "I figured he was talking about the sea in Asia."

Julian brought a finger to his lips as something clicked in his brain. He wasn't sure what, but there was something in the recesses of his mind about a hazy Red Sea. He was on to something. He turned his attention back to the brothers, looking from one to the other. "Anything else?"

"Nothing." They both squirmed and reaffirming their lack of any further knowledge, over and over.

The commander looked at the two sculls with disdain, then turned back to Rankin who still hadn't moved. He snapped his fingers toward Captain Enriquez, and one glare at Rankin had her also by his side.

"They are of no further use, Captain. Dispose of them."

Sub-Commander Rankin still stood on shaky legs with her bugged-out eyes staring at the lifeless body of the big, red-headed man. Julian needed to do something before she had a visible breakdown. "Sub-Commander Rankin," he said.

It took a few seconds for her to respond. "Yes, Commander."

"Find Drew Sherman. Bring him to me. I will be on the other side of the clearing by that fallen tree."

"Right away, Commander." With that, she skirted the dead body, her legs carrying her off toward the soldiers under the maple.

Julian looked at his watch as he walked toward the dead log sustaining the fungus and insect life thriving over its rotting surface. There was another 30 minutes before he could leave this plane and head back home. He was anxious to research the hazy Red Sea previously mentioned. It was important—almost as important as getting this comical troupe back on the right track to find Daniel. Even more critical was finding Nolan Harrison and discovering why he was so important. *Why does this troubadour, Daniel, go to so much trouble for a scull?*

The sound of footsteps through the soggy, knee-length grass broke through Julian's thoughts. Turning, he faced Sherman and Enriquez, while Rankin stayed a little further in the distance.

Julian cocked his head toward Drew Sherman. "You're supposed to be the best. That's why I asked for your help. Quite honestly, I'm sick of excuses, so let's pass on the reasons why we're no further ahead today than we were four days ago. I want to know what we do from here."

The rain had stopped. Drew Sherman removed his hat, hitting it several times against his thigh covered by the bottom of a long, wet coat. The water droplets shook off the hat, and he put it back on his head. "We need to backtrack. I thought there were less tracks a while back, but it's hard to tell in this water-logged terrain. There were a few spots where it would have been possible for someone to veer off the path without being noticed. I can find them."

"With all due respect to your skills, Sherman, you missed them on the way up here. What makes you think you can find their tracks on your way back?"

"I was asked to find five people crashing through the woods. I found them, or, at least, three of them. Now, obviously, the task is to find two people who are hiding their tracks. That is altogether different. Knowing that, I'll find them."

"Excellent!" Julian turned his eyes to Captain Enriquez. "Once you find the hidden tracks, send a runner to notify me, so I can come back to this god forsaken plane and ensure there are no more mistakes. Now get this squad up and moving. You're wasting time."

"Yes, Sir!"

For a moment Julian thought Captain Enriquez was mocking him with his sharp salute. He opened his mouth, but both men had already turned, moving to rouse the squad. Julian found a clear spot on the decaying log and sat down. Sub-Commander Rankin came and sat beside him. She still hadn't said a word since he interrogated the prisoners. Her clothes were still soaking wet, but with the warmth of the sun beating on their position, suddenly, the strong scent of urine filled the air.

Julian didn't look at Rankin, realizing—damn, she pissed herself! He looked away, trying unsuccessfully to hold back his grin.

Chapter 15

Nolan awoke from a deep sleep with his eyes blinking in an effort to stay open. They focused on the ceiling, and as he saw the rough-hewed beams, he jolted upright, his eyes pressed open as wide as saucers. He expected to see the white-tiled ceiling of his room in the fire station. However, his momentary disorientation was short lived, as he now recognized the cabin and the sounds of breathing coming from his two, still-slumbering companions. The faintest rays of light flickering through the east window brought the single room out of the night's darkness. The sun hadn't fully risen, but it painted the sky ahead of it with curved, flowing strokes of orange and red, resembling the roll of the sea before the tide.

His childhood bedroom had a window which also faced east. He'd seen every type of sunrise in his growing years and recalled the different moods of the sky. From shades of purple and gray as the light tried to pass through the overcast, to bright-yellow beams shooting heavenly light through the holes in the fluffy morning clouds, to the skies resembling what he saw outside the cabin window now, his awe of nature's ability to paint had not faded so many years later.

Nolan remembered when he was a child of eight, he painted a sunrise in art class. The orange and red scene was his favorite, so that's what went on the paper. The fact the technique they had to use was finger painting gave him an excuse for the poor quality—at least that was what he told his father when he gave it to him. Nolan remembered the smile on his father's face. Years later, he knew it was pride more than happiness, but as a young child, the smile meant more to Nolan than anything. When his father had it framed and placed on the wall in the hallway, it brought even more joy to the young artist, especially when his father made a point of showing it to every single person passing through the front entryway.

He missed his father.

Nolan was distracted by a shuffle of covers in Daniel's bed and saw his mentor was awake and propped up on his elbows.

"You were deep in thought," the older man said.

"It's quiet and in the quiet, the mind can wander. I was thinking of my childhood."

"I would love to hear about it," Daniel said as he sat further up in the bed.

"It's boring. You don't really want to know."

"Nolan." Daniel's eyes caught the younger mans' with true compassion. "I really would like to know more about you."

The persuasive tone convinced Nolan, and before he knew it, he was rambling on and on, beginning with his birth and progressing through every year of his early life. It included girlfriends, school fights, disappointments and proud moments. Nothing was left out. It was an hour later when Nolan finished the biography with the description of the painting in the hallway. Daniel hadn't said a word, and Germaine, who awoke halfway through, had also listened with quiet respect.

"Your father raised a fine son," Daniel said. "I hope to meet him one day."

Eyes moist with emotion, Nolan looked at his mentor. "Do you think I'll ever see him again?"

"You have a new life now, Nolan, but one cannot forget the past. It will always be there, but there is so much danger that lies ahead. Who knows if we will be alive a month from now? But let's make this pledge right now." Daniel's eyes came alive as the morning light reflected sky-blue in them. "When the danger is past, we will visit your father together—you and I."

"You would do that for me?"

"It is a small thing compared to what I have asked of you," Daniel replied.

A wide smile crossed Nolan's face. "Done then! The pledge is sealed!" His lifted spirits gave him life. "Let's go then. We have a lot of work to do today," he said as he bounced up off the mattress.

Daniel laughed. "Not so quickly, my young buck! We need to eat."

"We will need the frying pan," Germaine said in a sleepy voice. "It's still outside, full of rotten fish—I'm sure."

Daniel rose out of bed, stretching up and rearwards with his fingertips just missing the beams. "Do we have more of those instant eggs—the freeze-dried stuff? It's really not that bad at all."

"Loads and loads." Nolan grinned.

Returning from the front door, Germaine was scratching his head, a confused look on his face. He pushed the frying pan out to where the other two men could see it. It was, in fact, full, as he had predicted, but the salmon was gone. Hanging out one end of the pan were two long, fur-covered legs. Hanging off the other end were the long ears, unmistakably identifying the contents as a jack-rabbit.

Howling with laughter, Nolan danced around the cabin. He made several loops, making sure both Germaine and Nolan understood this was *his* forest, and he understood the animals within it. He stopped for a moment in front of the older man, grasping both of his shoulders. "He's not so smart. He has pride," Nolan mocked while bouncing his head back and forth. "He'll never take food from a human. Hah!" He released the shoulders, jumping to his left and danced three more gleeful rounds of the room.

Daniel looked at Germaine. "This cabin suddenly feels confining for three grown—" He raised a questioning eyebrow at Nolan "—men."

Germaine set aside the rabbit and went about making the eggs for all three of them.

A strange aroma brought Nolan down from his gloating high. Raising his nose, he sniffed the air. "What's that? It smells damn good!"

"It's dried kateer meat," Germaine responded. "I brought some with me from Crann Bith."

Daniel's eyes lit up. "Food from my home-world!" His eyes turned to Nolan who had settled by the eating table. "The taste of kateer is much like pig, but the beast itself is more similar to a boar, having the same intimidating, curved tusks. However, the kateer is slightly larger than a boar, standing almost three feet high at the shoulder."

"As long as it tastes as good as pork," Nolan said as he watched the plate put before him by Germaine, with eggs on one side and fried kateer on the other. His fingers, directed by his empty stomach, crammed alternating forkfuls of egg and salty kateer meat into his mouth. Albeit with a little more elegance, the other two companions cleared their plates, just behind Nolan's pace.

After breakfast, Daniel didn't have to give Germaine instructions. He knew his routine for the day. Check the perimeter. Check the direction where the Kaezzarites would eventually come, and check the snares.

Straightening out his ponytail, Germaine asked, "The creature in the frying pan has good meat on it, but not enough for three. I take it there are more about?"

"That there are," Nolan answered. "But they are quick. It might take you some time to catch one," he warned.

"Expanding his chest, Germaine turned toward the Earthman. "My birth name is Tulak~Raul. I am a leader of one hundred warriors from the clan of Shent on my home world. My father, Raul~Cor, better known as Raul Fire-Eyes, was a leader of one thousand." He pulled open his shirt, revealing six diagonal cuts. Three were on the left pectoral muscle and three on the right. "He put these here when I passed the six tests of manhood. I wear them with honor." His dark eyes turned to Daniel. "My mentor took me in eight years ago, bringing me to his world. At my request he renamed me and calls me Germaine now. On his world, which I now call my own, I trained intensely in the art of fighting and the skill of survival, receiving my silver band in acknowledgment. Two more bands, and I will match my mentor." During his talk he hadn't blinked—until now, using the pause to better highlight his point. His words were clear and direct with every syllable emphasized. "The quick feet of an oversized rodent will not be a problem."

Nolan grinned. "Then I'm looking forward to rabbit stew for dinner."

Germaine jutted his chin out. "The best you've ever had." He turned, walking toward the front entry. "That's if you're not too weary after your training." The words faded as the leader of one hundred was already out the door and on the march for rabbit in the light drizzle which had just begun to fall.

A sly chuckle came from under Daniel's thick, blonde moustache.

Raising both eyebrows, Nolan looked even younger, taking ten years off his 28. "What?"

"That look of sweet innocence won't work on me, my young friend. You are as clever as a fox." Daniel grinned, and his eyes sparkled with admiration.

"Well, I do have a craving for rabbit stew."

"I saw that, and if you would have asked Germaine to make rabbit stew, he would have quite curtly reminded you of your place as apprentice amongst the three of us."

Nolan's face muscles converted the look of innocence to one filled with a smart-assed smile.

Daniel waggled a finger at the younger man. "Your mind is quick when it wants to be. With a few subtle, but oh so clever words, you all but challenged Germaine to make the stew. Right now, the pursuit of rabbits is probably more important than those cuts of honor his father placed on his chest."

Looking coyly at Daniel, Nolan asked, "Do you like rabbit stew?"

Daniel, quick as a whip, rose and chased Nolan out of the cabin, swearing and cursing in English intermingled with other foreign languages. The look in the old man's eyes and the tone of the words were enough to affirm the less than noble nature of the profanity.

The training was more difficult on that day. The pattern was similar with a mix of mental psychic and physical exercises. The mentor changed the order of the three disciplines, making it more difficult for Nolan to keep his composure and focus, but he was learning to adjust. He knew he was progressing.

Nolan told Daniel he could see the Athar without his assistance, bringing pride to the older man's blue eyes, but it only gave Daniel more resolve to push Nolan even harder. Now, when Nolan invoked his mind's eye view of the Athar, Daniel would distract him. The twig, having become heavily sodden with moisture, would flick Nolan's back, and the Athar would be lost. The clapping of Daniel's weathered hands had the same result.

They ran even further than the day before, notwithstanding the treacherous, rain-slick terrain. Even here, Daniel would ask Nolan to find the Athar in his mind, and at first it was impossible, as his focus always returned to the ache in his leg muscles. Daniel even told him to focus on the ache so that he could relax his mind. It took Nolan six laps of the cabin trail before he realized the words from Daniel were also a ploy. It was just another distraction, but despite it, Nolan knew he was learning.

The rain finally stopped. Daniel didn't break for lunch, and he gave Nolan very little water. The depletion caused stresses on different parts of the younger man's body. It was another test to see if he could hold the Athar— and he did. As the sun retreated beyond the mountains, leaving the sky with threads of red and orange, Nolan had learned to focus. None of his mentor's distractions broke his concentration. This, along with the ability to stay relaxed, were two of the keys to harnessing the energy of the Athar Daniel spoke of. He was beginning to master both, but confidence was still an open issue yet to be resolved.

That night, Germaine indeed made the best rabbit stew Nolan ever tasted. There were some spices in the mix he hadn't tasted before, and Germaine found carrots and potatoes in an overgrown garden, adding to the aroma of the mixture as it cooked. It filled the cabin with an earthy scent, forcing their mouths to water and for their minds to suffer with the thought they had to wait for the meat to fully cook.

"Patience. It will be ready momentarily," Germaine reassured them.

Nolan, with his wrists resting on his chest, rolled his fingers over top of each other in anticipation. "I wish we had some fresh bread. As good as this is going to be, a thick slice of bread to sop up the gravy would be a fitting end to the meal." In his mind, Nolan had already eaten the meal several times.

"Use your fingers if you have to." Daniel grinned as he lifted his nose to inhale the scent torturing his stomach. "Your lack of manners would be quite understandable."

Daniel and Nolan watched the skilled cook. With their heads tilted down, their eyes angled up as they slid back and forth in the sockets, watching every move Germaine made. The demeanor of the two hungry men was reminiscent of a dog watching its loving owner cooking Christmas dinner, hoping for the odd scrap to be thrown its way.

Finally, Germaine determined the stew was ready, and all three men enjoyed every bite of the hearty meal. Nolan and the other two men did, in fact, use their fingers to clean their bowls of every drop of the rich gravy. With their bellies now satisfied, they all leaned back on the closest, softest article which would suffice as a pillow. Their eyelids were heavy from the exertions of the day—except for Nolan.

"That really was the best stew I've eaten," Nolan said to Germaine who was sprawled on the couch. "You've proven yourself master of the rabbits in this forest. Their quickness was not an issue, and somehow, you even found vegetables." He had a curious smile on his face.

"As quick as my legs are, my mind is even quicker," Germaine replied. "It would make sense for who ever lived here to have a vegetable garden. It didn't take me long to find it, even though it was overgrown. Some animals found it as well—your wolf, I would imagine."

Nolan's mind went to the amber wolf eyes he saw several times during the day. The wolf was always there in the distance, watching their training exercises. He'd seen wolves before, but not for an extended period of time like this. He got to know those amber eyes, sensing a curiosity there, sometimes overlaid with jovial humor. What was curious to Nolan was what he didn't see, and that was fear. Considering the increasing number of humans threatening their space, most of the timber wolves had moved north and out of the forest. Hunting permits for elk and deer abounded, and every few years there was a controlled kill of these animals. It wasn't uncommon for the odd wolf to be the result of a hunter's so-called accident. Wolves had reason to fear man, but this wolf wasn't afraid. He hoped in times of the danger Daniel foretold in his words, his own eyes would be as resolute and brave as the half-eared wolf. "The wolf does what he has to do to survive, as we do, but his rabbit and vegetables were not as well prepared as ours. That really was the best stew I've eaten," Nolan said.

Germaine smiled genuinely at the younger man, and his humility showed in his response of silence.

"Did you take one of your pills?" Daniel asked Nolan.

"Yes. With the meal."

"Good. Now that your level of expertise has begun to show through, we must keep you from having another wild dream. Who knows what size rift you could open with the training and knowledge you now have? The pill keeps you on the edge with the ability to view the Athar, but it would take an extraordinary effort to penetrate it."

Nolan turned on his side, lying on the mattress with his elbow bent, so his head rested on his palm. "You don't think I could control the power without the pill?"

Daniel shrugged. "I don't know, but I would hate to find out the hard way. When we are ready to hop, the pills will need to stop at least 12 hours prior to."

Although Nolan understood the sensical words, a momentary look of disappointment crossed his face.

"Don't get me wrong, Young Nolan. You have made amazing progress, but there is still much to do, and that will be for tomorrow."

Nolan appreciated the praise, but he was an admitted student of the human mind. He questioned people's actions often, especially the small gestures of word or form many would deem insignificant. Was the praise genuine, or was it a motivational tool to build Nolan's effort and trust—or both? The evaluation seemed cold and somewhat calculating, but Nolan's mind would veer down that path from time to time. He even questioned himself on his praise of Germaine's stew. It was very good, but he suspected the praise was also to bring him closer to the strange, off-world warrior. Notwithstanding the praise of his mentor, his own doubt about his integrity, sparked disappointment in himself. Rolling to his back, he pulled his blanket up around his neck. "There's much to do tomorrow, then," he said. "Good night," and with that his eyes closed.

The next two days were much the same as the previous two. Germaine would leave early in the morning to perform his patrol, scouting the area for any signs of the Kaezzarites. He would search in the direction he expected them to come, but he occasionally would make a complete round of the perimeter. He carried a loathing for the Kaezzarites, but he was wary, knowing them to be clever. It was unlikely they would amble in and knock on the front door.

Daniel continued to train Nolan. The younger man's body grew stronger as did his mind. Now, when Nolan invoked the Athar, the markers would light brightly in his mind, calling him to their locations. There was an underlying urge pulling him to the red and yellow flashes, and Daniel explained it as the intuitive sense purebloods have for the Athar. Nolan knew the only thing keeping him from moving to those locations were the little, red pills.

On the third day, Germaine left early in the morning on his foray, when the sun was rising, chasing away the orange hue to be replaced by a bright-blue, cloudless sky. The birds sung their melody infused with the higher pitched chirps of the hatchlings now hungry for nourishment and the chance to call the forest their own.

Nolan had his shirt off. The warmer day and the exertion of the exercises, created a sheen of sweat on his chest. Suddenly, he turned his head from side to side. The wolf wasn't there. The wolf had become more comfortable with the three men, but especially Nolan. It made a habit of lying on the edge of the clearing, not 15 yards from the position they used for training. When Nolan went on his run, the wolf would mirror his movements, keeping a short distance from him but paralleling his course through the dense brush.

Nolan communicated with the wolf. Their eyes looked into each other's many times now. Even though it was from a distance, both saw similar traits of honor and respect. In an odd way, man and beast became bonded. That is why Nolan thought it odd, in the midday sun the wolf preferred, it was nowhere in sight.

The shrill tone pierced the forest, interrupting Nolan's thoughts.

Daniel, who was just rising to his feet, froze for an instant, his blue eyes opened wide. On his haunches, he twisted his head from side to side, probing the surrounding brush and forest. Seeing nothing out of place, his eyes turned back to Nolan. Their intensity surprised Nolan, causing him to rock back, falling onto the wood stump.

The older man's voice was as crisp as the mountain air. "That was a chilo shell."

"Shit!"

"It might just be an animal, but we are not going to take chances. Move quickly. You have one minute to get your things in your pack." The older man straightened his long legs, turning to the front door of the cabin.

Nolan followed his mentor. "Where are we going? Shouldn't we wait for Germaine?"

"Germaine can take care of himself. We need to make our way a distance from the cabin, where we will watch—and wait."

"Are you…"

Daniel's face flashed up. "This isn't the time for questions!" His hands were quickly pressing clothes and other personal items into his pack. "You only have a minute. Pack your things quickly." The older man moved to Germaine's pack, jamming the warrior's belongings into its confines. He slung one pack over each shoulder, then his feet took him swiftly to the door. Seeing the urgency in Daniel's eyes, Nolan threw his things in his pack and ran after the older man. Daniel's finger lifted, pointing north up the inclining terrain toward the forest of fir trees.

The two men set a quick pace. First, they moved along the path they made from their daily run, then, after one hundred yards, they veered true north, winding their way up the rocky terrain. Long grass and even the odd fern dotted the mountainside in the open area between their small encampment and the forest just ahead of them. They felt uncomfortable, but the dense forest would bring safety and a vantage point to view the cabin a few hundred yards below.

It was just another 20 yards to the tree line. They needed to skirt a short, ten-foot-high crag of rock jutting out from the side of the mountain. It was the last obstacle before the comforting envelope of trees. Panting for breath, their muscles strained with the uphill trek. They looked behind them every few seconds, fully expecting to see men following along their tracks.

As they came around the edge of the rock outcropping, Nolan took one last glance back downhill, and then turned his gaze forward. He stopped in his tracks, seeing two men blocking their path. *Kaezzarites!* he thought. Their faces were tired, framed by long, uncombed hair. They looked as if the pursuit had sapped much of their strength. Nolan thought about fighting, but the guns the two men carried were pointed squarely at them. The guns looked similar to a small machine gun except they had a strange muzzle on the end of the barrel. He saw a glow of green in his peripheral view as

Daniel's shield formed, blanketing his body in a crackling layer of energy.

The Kaezzarite with the thick beard spoke, his narrowed eyes looking squarely at Daniel. "Stand down, or we'll kill your friend."

Every world must have a figure akin to Satan. Right now, Daniel, clad in his long leather coat with his face shrouded by the rim of the weathered, leather hat and only the bright-blue eyes ripping through the green haze, fit such a devilish description.

The two Kaezzarites looked at each other furtively, but their weapons didn't waiver.

Daniel's shield disappeared with electrostatic popping sounds emitting from the dispersion. He said nothing as the two armed men inched toward them.

In a gruff voice, the bearded man said, "Hands on your head. Intertwine your fingers. If I see that shield again, I'll kill him." He nodded the tip of the laser rifle toward Nolan.

The bearded man sidestepped forward, closer to Daniel. The other Kaezzarite kept his distance with the gun trained on the two prisoners. His eyes were small and untrusting with the pupils vibrating back and forth in his nervousness. Without warning, his eyes opened wide. The whistle of the knife through the air preceded the *thump* as the steel sliced through flesh and bone into the man's back. Before the man's dead body hit the ground, a wild scream came from above. Germaine had launched himself off the outcropping and his other knife was held backhanded as he flew down toward the second Kaezzarite. The unfortunate man barely had time to look up, seeing the steel glint in the sun as it slashed across the front of his neck.

Nolan wondered what it felt like. He was not thinking of the pain of a cut or the surprise of being bested, but the knowledge, in your last seconds of life, that you were dying—that in the next few moments your breaths would stop, and you would be nothing but spent energy lying in the soil you would soon be part of.

The man dropped his gun. His hand came up to grip his neck, instinctively trying to hold back the blood flowing deep-red through his fingers. His hollow eyes, still filled with shock, stared at Daniel before they rolled back in his head. Then, his legs buckled, and he fell to the ground.

"There could be more nearby!" Germaine hissed. "Let's move!"

Daniel threw Germaine his pack, and the three men raced for the tree line which was only seconds away. A long dead, moss-covered log lay on its side in their path. Germaine and Daniel hit the log first, whereby they both jumped to clear the rotting wood. Nolan saw the large net thrown down from the trees, but it was too late. Both men were airborne, flying toward the strange, yellow, glowing mesh. It crackled and popped as it collided with the green energy field both men instinctively invoked.

All this transpired in only a brief second as Nolan tried to stop his momentum toward the log. He didn't see the fist, but he felt it lash out from the darkness of the forest, hitting him in the side of his head. He wavered. Through hazy eyes, he saw his companions being subdued by several assailants until finally, he fell into unconsciousness.

Chapter 16

Sixty-two caskets filled with the bodies of the Kaezzarites that had died while defending the state from the Celtae attack, gently rocked on the *River of Passing*. Appropriately named, the 50-yard-wide river was used exclusively for the ceremonial last journey of the Kaezzarite dead as they moved from life to their last resting place in Lake Fuego.

The river, devoid of waves, was perfectly straight over its half-mile length. As such, it would be more accurately defined as a canal, but who really wants their body to have its last rites on a canal? Consequently, "river" was the Kaezzarite society's unanimous definition of the body of water.

Custom required family and friends to pull the air-tight casket from either side of the river, up its length, using the golden twisted ropes anchored to hooks set into either side of the beautifully painted boxes.

Good coffin artists charged top cort to re-create the life story of the dead person on the casket. Typically, the artist would be contracted when the person was 20 years old, and during the following years, he would paint a colorful history of the purchaser as the events of time unfolded. As such, by the amount of painting, it was easy to estimate how old and influential the person was. Today's sight was sad. Very few of the coffins were painted over the halfway mark along their length. Since the war had been going on for so long, the average age of death for a Kaezzarite was 52 years. Most of those lying lifeless in the motionless, cool water were closer to half that age.

The State ceremony was just beginning. The somber silence was appropriate, and even the contrasting, vivid beauty of the landscaped gardens bordering both shores of the clear, blue river could not distract the family's minds from the death floating before them. For this tragedy, the 62 caskets were linked together with shorter, gold ropes, creating a diamond pattern. The outer caskets were the only ones to have longer ropes reaching the shore. Groups of family members dotted the shore on either side at 50-yard intervals, and each group was ready to take their turn pulling the parade of death.

Julian sat in the bleachers set on either side of the river, just behind the gardens in the area reserved for Watch Command. He was surrounded by a sea of blue uniforms—proof the Watch was well represented. Sitting in the second row with the other sector watch commanders and just behind Adrian Korlis, he watched the procession begin to move. Family members used one of three instruments: a bell, a thin drum or a tambourine. They shook or beat each instrument in unison, matching the slow stride of their legs as they pulled their beloved on their way to their final resting place.

Turning his head to the side, Julian saw the other state agencies also well represented. On his left were the tan uniforms of the Exploratory Corp., and on their left were the royal-blue uniforms of the Engineers. He smirked at the thin caps they wore on their heads. *Always trying to be different,* he thought. Leaning forward and turning his gaze to the right, he saw the sea of black. These were the Kaezzar military. They were one of the best trained forces in the Athar and had been given the nickname *Black Swarm* by those who felt the power of their burst or the touch of their steel. The Black Swarm were just as proficient with both.

Although both men and women held equal rank in all the service organizations of Kaezzar, the two rows of rust-colored uniforms directly in front of the Black Swarm were primarily filled by men. The State Guard were the fighting elite. Their only task in life was to protect the state leader and his family, who at this time sat in a private box directly in front of their guard.

As the procession of coffins moved further up river, Julian considered his place in the sea of uniforms. Each group had their pride and wore their colors well. Valor, bravery and even heroism was the goal of so many, but none of the groups held the power of Watch Command since Watch Command controlled the Athar. Nothing moved without their approval and knowledge. All roads passed through Command, and Julian knew someday soon the Athar would belong to him.

Squinting, he peered down to the far end of the river, seeing the first caskets being pulled out and rolled up specially constructed ramps onto the terrain transports. The arid salt flats covering most of this world were not suitable for burials, so alternatively, for years, the dead were given their last rites along the River of Passing before being transported to Lake Fuego. Once there, the transports were backed up to a long ceramic slide, and the caskets were tipped into the molten lava. This was the Kaezzarite version of returning to the dirt from which all life began.

Julian's pocket phone vibrated. He frowned, annoyed at the distraction. Pulling it half out of his pocket, he saw the two green flashing keys. His curiosity grew considering he gave only a very few people the emergency code that would set it off. As much as he wanted to answer the call, he couldn't leave the ceremony without being noticeable. He cancelled the signal and shoved the phone gruffly back into his pocket.

It took another 45 minutes for the ceremony to finish, then another 15 minutes for the State leader to give his closing remarks to the civilians who crammed into the bleachers on the other side of the river. He promised a swift response to the attack. The comment made Julian chuckle, for three days had already passed since the Celtae attack.

The phone vibrated again. Julian cursed under his breath, seeing the same two flashing lights. He smacked the disconnect button and all but threw the receiver back into his pocket. But thankfully, he could see the ceremony was about to finish. The throng of spectators rose in unison and made their way to the exits. Pushing and squeezing his thin body through the crowd, Julian squirmed to the MagTrak station just south of the river and found a quiet corner where he could inconspicuously discover the source of the emergency call. As he pulled out the phone to review the call history, the phone vibrated again with the same two lights being energized.

Julian's thumb slid over the top of the phone, pressing the "receive" button. "Yes," was all he said.

"Captain Cool?" a voice responded in a questioning tone.

One corner of his mouth turned down in irritation. Julian knew it was Luis Ortez. "I told you to only use this number if you had an emergency!" he said while spittle coated the speaker.

"My apologies, Captain Cool, but I've found something you will want to see right away."

Julian looked at his watch. It was 3:30 in the afternoon. "Tie line 4-31B, scramble code 3-alpha at exactly 4:30," was all he said before he clicked the receiver off. As Julian headed back into the throng and down into the MagTrak levels, he considered the investment he'd made in Luis. Perhaps it was finally going to pay off.

He made good time on the way back to his apartment with ten minutes remaining before Luis was scheduled to call. Kicking off his shoes, he headed for the kitchen and poured himself a cool ferequa. Ferequa was light-blue in color and was made from the fermented berries of the mallow fruit which grew wild in the rainforest on the north side of Lake Fuente. *It was considered a woman's drink, but he didn't give a shit,* he thought as he topped up the glass.

Walking to his couch, he lowered himself into the soft cushions. His eyes settled on the file folder on the table in front of him. So far it was a good day. *Perhaps Luis will surprise me and give me something I can work with,* he considered. Reaching for the file, Julian's index finger flicked the top cover of the folder open, revealing the picture of the man who yesterday he knew as Daniel, but today he knew as Daniel Barrymore Dupuis. His bio disclosed his history as a retired explorer from the city of Bailemor on the world of Crann Bith.

The hazy, Red Sea, which had been brought to his attention by the captives on Earth, had definitely rung a bell in Julian's mind. It finally clicked when he remembered reading of Bailemor. It was a Celtae city which Kaezzar had not had a confrontation with in 80 years, but the battles of that era were bloody enough to make it to the history books. From there, it was easy. The historical words described the city of Bailemor as the only living area on their planet, while the rest of the planet was dead as the result of a uranium-based attack that left a radioactive fog. Mixed with red sand particles, the deadly combination covered most of the planet's surface.

Since the search parameters had been narrowed down, it didn't take the Watch Command's automated database search program long to match the face in the picture to the one in the security file. There was quite a bit of description regarding the man known as Daniel. He was a veteran of many military campaigns, and as he grew on in years, he joined the Exploration Services until he retired two years ago. At least, that was the information documented by the Toltec spies in Bailemor. This heightened Julian's curiosity. Daniel Dupuis was highly skilled—a grizzled veteran who couldn't conceivably have an interest in a scull on Earth. There must be much more to Nolan Harrison than meets the eye for Mr. Dupuis to show such an active interest.

A green light began to flash on the upper left corner of the video screen on the far wall, followed shortly thereafter by two monotone electronic beeps. Picking up his keyboard, he pressed the button connecting the computer feed. It immediately asked for his identification number and password which he promptly entered. His personal home page came up and, from that, he called up his security clearance file. Mouthing the characters, he keyed in the tie line number 4-31B, followed by the scramble code 3-alpha. He moved the cursor overtop of the left flashing light, then clicked "enter." Immediately, he saw the shiny face of Luis Ortez, his forehead already breaking out in a sweat.

"Don't look around like that Luis. It's a computer, so no one else can see you," Julian scoffed.

"Of course, of course." Luis used his finger to press his glasses higher on his nose and leaned closer to peer into the monitor on his end of the connection.

"What do you have for me? It must be good for you to use the emergency channel."

"You will not be disappointed," Luis said. Not heeding Julian's advice, he looked furtively from side to side. "As you know, I've been monitoring Adrian Korlis's phone line. There was a curious call the night of the raid on the generator station. It came from the station to his private line at home."

Julian tapped his fingers on the keyboard. "I'm sure there is more."

Luis continued with his eyes wide, showing his excitement. "As you know, the steam generator plant is not a good place to work. The heat can be unbearable even in the somewhat controlled inner confines of the main buildings. Consequently, the Department of Penal Affairs provides the labor to man the facility, overseen by guards. That's why the very quick phone call surprised me. The caller said 'Prisoner M0284 was uninjured,' and then the call disconnected."

"Tell me how prisoner M0284 interests me."

"It will indeed interest you. I hacked into the warden's computer and pulled M0284's profile. The inmate is named Jelan Tulis, but that is unimportant." Luis waved his hand and moved himself on. "What is important is his birth date. He was born on the forty-second day of the second quarter of the Kaezzar year 2034."

Julian grew impatient. "Do you tell me this so I can send him a birthday greeting!"

"No," Luis said as he shrunk back from the screen. "But it's an important piece of information."

"How so?"

"The day before, I took your advice and hacked into Adrian Korlis's computer and searched his files. I read about his brother."

"Julian said sarcastically. "Yes—a sad story, but he died a hero. He was lost during a strike against a Celtae world three years ago."

"*Supposedly* killed."

"What do you mean?" Julian leaned forward in anticipation.

"Adrian's brother—his birth date was on the forty-second day of the second quarter of 2034. It's the *same* birth date as prisoner M0284."

Julian sat in shock for a moment, then threw himself back against the couch, his legs stretching forward under the table as he put together the pieces of information. Jelan Tulis *was* Adrian Korlis's brother! His face, covered with a wide grin, looked up at the ceiling. In it, he imagined Adrian's bearded face. "I finally have you!" he yelled, raising a fist at the apparition. "Your ass is mine!"

Chapter 17

Nolan pried his eyes open. He saw only darkness. Instantly, his heart raced. Feeling the ache in his head, he jumped to a conclusion. Remembering the impact to the side of his head, he thought the force of the blow damaged his sight. Lying on his back, he gingerly turned onto his side, hearing the creak of the floorboards under him. With his vision beginning to clear, he saw fuzzy shapes and figures—two of each. Shaking his head, he cleared the double-vision and, to his relief, realized the darkness was due to the nighttime hour. He must have been out for a long time.

"He's awake."

Nolan heard the voice from behind him. His pupils adjusted to the lower light level, as the dark sky was lit a midnight-blue by the full moon each time it slid past a cloud. He realized he was back at the cabin, lying on the wood planks of the porch. As he tried to right himself, he found it wasn't the ache in his head making his movements difficult. Rather, his hands were bound behind his back, and a mesh net was draped over his body. He was able to squirm around far enough to see one of the Kaezzarites standing by the door.

At that moment, another person came out of the cabin, walked over and peered down at Nolan's prone form. "Let's keep this simple. I am Captain Enriquez. You have an energy mesh draped over you. Try and hop from this plane, and it will join your body's energy. End result—you will be dead. If you try to run, Raul—" He nodded his chin at the man by the door "—will shoot you. End result—you will be dead." He moved to one knee, leaning closer over Nolan. "I don't want to hear your words. Just indicate your understanding. If you nod your head up and down, that means you understand. If you nod your head from side to side, that means you don't understand. In that case, I will shoot you. End result—you will be dead."

Nolan nodded his head up and down.

Satisfied, Captain Enriquez rose, pushing up off his knee as he looked to Raul. "Put him with the others, then return to your watch by the door."

Nolan watched the man salute before he came over to his position and, with a hand under his armpit, pulled him to his feet. He almost fell when Raul pushed him in the back. Anger flared in Nolan's eyes as he turned, but the muzzle of the gun subdued his mood.

"Over there," Raul said, nudging the gun in the direction of the storage shed.

Nolan's eyes adjusted to the darkness. He saw both Germaine and Daniel sitting cross-legged just to the left of the shed. A guard sat beside them, and to Nolan's chagrin, he was sitting on Nolan's wooden tree stump. Ominously, the guard's gun was at the ready, hanging from a shoulder strap and supported across his thighs. Once they were close to the location of the other two prisoners, Nolan felt a sharp push in his back for the second time. This time, it sent him sprawling across the red-needled bed covering the forest floor. He rolled to a sitting position beside Daniel, feeling the needles stuck to his cheek after having raked along the ground.

"Another Celtae scum for you to watch," Raul said. He turned back to the cabin, but not before he spat on the ground as if the action would cleanse his mouth after uttering the enemy's name.

There was a look of warning in Daniel's eyes as Nolan looked at the older man. The message was clear. This was not the time to talk. Daniel looked unharmed, but Germaine hadn't fared as well. The Celtae warrior's face was swollen, and there was a deep gash over his left eye. The Kaezzarites didn't like the fact Germaine killed two of their comrades, he concluded. The evidence could be seen on the ground not far from the porch of the cabin, where two body bags were laid.

A block of light streamed across the ground as the cabin door was thrust open. The light from the lanterns in the cabin surrounded the burly shape of a man who quickly began striding to their position. Once sighting him, the guard rose from the tree stump and met the newcomer halfway across the distance to the cabin. Nolan saw they were having a discussion, joking and laughing in a casual mood now that they captured their quarry. The younger guard who just left them kept his gun pointed in the prisoner's direction, providing the illusion of performing his duties.

"This looks hopeless," Nolan said. "Why don't you two hop out of here?"

"This mesh keeps us from hopping, but even if we could, we would not leave you here. We have come too far to give up so easily," Daniel replied.

"The guard said something about not being able to hop with this mesh on, but it's beyond my understanding."

Daniel could not help but chuckle. They were in dire danger—perhaps mortal danger—and still his young apprentice had questions. "The mesh has a strong energy signature. A pureblood can transport to another plane, but if he tries to take another strong energy source with him, it is fatal. The two energy fields combine during the transposition, and when the signature re-materializes in the destination plane, usually it is as a grotesque, disfigured person. If he does not die instantly, the misplaced organs will usually be the factor killing him within minutes."

"Freaking hell. Shouldn't you have told me that earlier?" Nolan whispered.

"Perhaps. Since we do not have a lot of time right now, I will give you the crash course. All you need to know, assuming we somehow miraculously get out of this, is if you are going to hop, relieve yourself of all guns, batteries, explosives—any type of power source."

Germaine leaned forward, looking over at Nolan. "Being forgetful can be painful."

Nolan's eyebrows furrowed, and his mouth opened to respond, but he was interrupted by laughter from the two Kaezzar men. The older man from the cabin clapped the younger guard on the back before making his way toward the three prisoners.

The man came closer and took his place on the stump. Peeking out from behind the cloud cover, the sporadic moonlight lit his face. It was bearded and round with a long scar down the side. He said, "Good evening, gentlemen. My name is Drew Sherman, and it's my turn to keep watch on you. Please, no sudden movements. I thought I retired out of this business, so I'm a little out of practice. If I get frazzled, I might just start shooting everything up." He tapped the side of his laser rifle.

"I thought all Toltec fought until they died. An honorable death in battle is desired, not a long life ending with illness in a retirement home. Isn't that the way it goes?" Daniel probed.

"To most Toltec, and let's not forget the equally blood-thirsty Celtae, the war is an obsession. I had my fill of killing, seeing my friends and loved ones die around me. Perhaps there are other things to fight for other than just for the sake of fighting."

Daniel raised an eyebrow as his curiosity about the man grew.

"Many purebloods—Toltec or Celtae— would have you arrested for treason for your words alone."

Drew Sherman chuckled. "If you're ever in a position where you are holding a gun to my head as *your* prisoner, then I'll be worried."

Daniel joined Sherman in his laughter. "You don't seem like a Toltec. You have a sense of humor, and you let words other than those of war come from your mouth. On both accounts, you have merit."

What happened next was unbelievable to Nolan who was having difficulty understanding the mood of light banter. Drew Sherman nonchalantly scratched his neck. His shirt was pulled down by the action, revealing a small coin-size tattoo on the left side of his chest. Only momentarily visible and difficult to discern in the darkness, Nolan squinted, seeing a sword and a hammer within the small, round tattoo, but that wasn't the incredible part. Daniel also leaned forward, letting his shirt, that had ripped during his earlier struggle, fall open. Nolan's jaw dropped, first thinking the intermittent moonlight was playing tricks on his eyes. He closed them tight—then opened them wide, but it was still there. On Daniel's chest was the exact same tattoo!

Nolan didn't know what to do or say. His mind and pulse began to race, but he used his breathing skills to calm himself. He decided to use his father's teaching. "If you don't understand, it probably means you have not listened well enough." Consequently, he decided to stay quiet and do just that.

Drew Sherman's face remained emotionless. "I've heard there are people in all the races who speak of things other than war."

"Where there is smoke, there is usually fire. Perhaps it is more than a rumor," Daniel responded, choosing his words carefully. "Some even think there is hope for peace."

"Peace is only something I see in my dreams, from time to time," Sherman whispered.

Daniel looked up at Sherman. "I have dreams of the Three Keys."

The words caught Sherman off guard, and he froze for a second before responding. "The Three Keys? I recall that as a fairy tale with the only value being the amusement of children."

"Most science is folklore until proven true. If the First Key has been found, many people would change their opinion," the older man countered.

Sherman leaned forward and whispered, "You are close to finding such proof?"

Since Nolan was on the left of the line of three prisoners, he was the closest to Sherman. As Sherman leaned forward, he could feel his breath as the guard's gaze bore into Daniel.

"You speak in past tense. The First Key *is* found and closer than you think." Daniel returned the intense look.

Nolan had just about enough of the riddles. He knew Daniel was an expert, but it appeared this other man was just as competent in completely befuddling him. Across the small clearing the cabin door opened again. The guard who left was now returning with a bowl of food in his hand, and the other hand was maneuvering a spoon from it to his mouth.

Drew Sherman rose and moved the stump he was sitting on closer to the cabin as the incoming guard moved to within ear shot. "You will be able to see them better from this position. He then walked behind the trio and bent behind each of them. "The bonds are all secure," he said to the young guard.

Nolan watched Drew Sherman walk back to the cabin. The last few minutes puzzled him. The feeling was heightened by the smile he saw on Daniel's face, particularly since they were still in mortal danger. However, what Nolan didn't know, was, as Sherman checked Daniel's bonds, a small knife passed between them and was now curled tightly in the older man's fingers, the sharp edge vigorously working on the nylon bindings.

Across the clearing, Nolan's attention was caught by a movement just in front of the tall fir trees. He saw a shimmering oval rippling in opaque waves. Someone was hopping in. A uniformed man appeared, wearing teal-blue pants and a like-colored, short jacket. He was bearded and short in stature. *Impatience* was the word that came to Nolan when he considered the look of the man.

As he re-materialized on Earth, once again, Julian looked up at the sky. It was blanketed with a darkness unusual to him as was the moon casting a low, reflected light down onto the surface of the planet. Across the clearing, he could see the three prisoners and the guard who jumped to attention once he caught sight of him. Pushing back the urge to move directly to the prisoners, he made his way to the cabin, pushing open the door. With a loud crack, it slammed against the wall on the other side of the rusty hinges. The laughter stopped immediately, as the occupants saw Julian, then they jumped to attention with each of them holding a salute. Julian held back his words as he slowly paced around the small room, his hands held behind his back with his fingers knit together. He made a complete circle of the small wooden structure before returning back to a position in front of the door. The rays from the fire lit up his face.

Turning to Enriquez, Julian said, "Count your personnel, Captain."

"Including myself, there are seven here, and the guard watching the prisoners would make eight."

"And when you left Kaezzar you had…"

"Ten men," the captain said through his frown. "There are two men in body bags outside, but then, you know that."

"That was the report I received, but I assumed I was wrong when I heard the laughter. I fully expected to see dancing girls when I opened the door."

"The team was happy the mission was accomplished successfully," Enriquez replied, dryly.

"Successfully? Three men of the original team were killed. Two more of your team were killed today. I've waited over a week for the capture— successful?" Julian's eyes looked through the man as if he was nothing. No more words came. He shook his head from side to side just as he would to a dog not being able to complete a simple task.

Enriquez moved the conversation along. "Would you like to interrogate the prisoners, Commander?"

Julian turned to the door. "Come along, Captain."

The cool night air chilled Julian. As he lifted the zipper tab on the front of his jacket, he looked up at Enriquez who had moved beside him. "Have you asked them any questions?"

"None, Commander. We assumed you would once again like to perform the function personally."

"Quite correct, Captain." Julian peered through the moonlit night at the three prisoners lined up in a neat row. "Looks familiar, does it not?" he said to Enriquez as he held his hand out, palm up.

Enriquez knew the drill, placing his laser pistol in Julian's hand. Transferring the gun into his belt, Julian walked toward the three men sitting cross-legged on the damp ground. *Daniel and Nolan, he needed. The third man was expendable,* he thought as he fingered the pistol once again, his mind calculating the probability of obtaining the answers he needed. The guard by the three prisoners shrank back and away from the killing he knew was coming. He retreated from the death he saw the commander settle into so easily already once this week. The rest of the squad was like minded. Enriquez kept his feet firmly planted, keeping his distance as did the other men who had not left the comfort of the cabin, although their laughter had subsided.

Julian crossed his arms across his chest. "We finally meet. You have led us on quite a chase." He stayed silent for a good minute as his eyes wandered from one prisoner to the other.

Casually, Julian lowered one hand, sliding his finger behind the trigger of the gun. "Enough pleasantries, then," he said as his eyes turned, looking squarely at Germaine. "Why did you come to this plane for this scull?" He flicked his head toward Nolan. "Think carefully before you answer."

Germaine's face was swollen, but he was able to speak through the fat lip. "Training and nuts."

"You will need to explain further." Julian's eyes narrowed, appraising Germaine.

Germaine's eyes turned a cold, dark black. "I came here to train sculls to cut off Kaezzarite nuts."

Julian's lips opened in a snarl with his teeth grinding together. His hand lifted, sliding the laser pistol out of his belt before releasing the safety.

Nolan heard the footfalls behind him. Immediately after, he felt the whoosh of air as the gray blur jumped through the space between his head and Daniel's. The wolf's wide front paws were already up, springing toward Julian. The thick back legs released their pent-up energy. Julian turned his head just in time to see the amber eyes and the fire in them, causing instant fear to course through every bone in his body. The hand holding the gun rose, the trigger pulled, but the impact of the wolf's weight on his chest sent the gun careening away. The blue laser beam fired into the sky like an emergency beacon as Julian was sent tumbling backward. He gasped for air to replace that knocked from his lungs.

The wolf landed on nimble legs, turning 90 degrees in a movement not seeming possible. In two quick strides, he was upon the young guard whose look of shock turned to one of horror as he felt the teeth crush down on his jugular. The ferocious bite ripped open the flesh as the animal's momentum carried its bulk past him. As the wide-eyed guard toppled, his hand glowed orange but sputtered out as the life force ebbed from his body.

Hearing the commotion, the men from the cabin ran out. An orange burst left the hand of one Kaezzarite, soaring toward the beast, finding naught but the displaced air from its quick, elusive movement.

Julian, dizzy from his tumble, lifted his gaze to see the creature diving toward his throat. Its lips were pulled back with sharp, blood-covered teeth poised in a threatening snarl. He just had time to raise his hand. Intense, stabbing pain shot through his arm, as the beast's teeth sank through the jacket into his flesh. Julian screamed as his arm was shaken like a rag doll. The incisors ripped the flesh. The wet feeling of blood dribbling along his arm brought a look of panic to his eyes. The panic drove Julian's instincts, and a flash of orange burst into view around his hand, sending the creature flying ten yards across the clearing. It allowed him the time to rise to his wobbly knees. The wolf was even quicker and back on its feet instantly. Another energy burst from the direction of the cabin just missed the wolf as its body was pushed to the left by strong, muscled legs.

In the commotion, the three prisoners freed themselves of their bonds. Nolan was just behind Daniel and Germaine, with their flight already well into the forest, when he turned to watch the struggle. Through two majestic fir tree trunks, he saw the wolf with the half ear, bathed in a ray of moonlight. Momentarily, the wolf looked into the forest, its amber eyes on fire and filled with life. Nolan saw pride and bravery in those eyes. The wolf knew an honorable death was near.

The wolf turned its head up, neck arching, as a deep growl began to form within it. Its front legs bent down as the guttural reverberations grew in intensity. Then, as its legs sprung to a straightened position and its mouth opened wide, the loudest of howl's burst across the black lips, echoing off the mountains. Amongst the echoes, other howls began. One—then a second and a third. Soon, the howls of many wolves reverberated throughout the surrounding forest. A howl would sound in the distance, followed by another. Each cracked the air as if it wasn't even ten feet away. The nocturnal sounds cascading through the forest gave the night an eerie coldness, freezing the Kaezzarites with fear. The men turned and stared into the darkness, unsure of their own safety.

The howls of his brothers and sisters motivated Half-Ear. He snapped his proud head to the side with a snarl and, once again, broke for Julian who was still fazed, kneeling on the damp ground.

Julian yelled, and the high-pitched plea for help startled the men of Red Squad back to reality. The men, fearing Julian's wrath more than the wolves, turned and began firing burst after burst at the beast. The first and second missed, but the third caught Half-Ear square in the side. It threw the wolf to the left of Julian who cowered with his eyes closed and both hands covering his face. Half-Ear rolled several times as his fur sizzled. Finally coming to rest, his eyes were open, and in his dead stare Nolan did not see fear or pain. It was a good death.

Daniel and Germaine had run a few yards ahead before they realized Nolan had stopped. Now that the struggle in the clearing was over, Daniel yelled back, "It's over. Let's go!"

Nolan didn't waste time, having seen enough of this death. Long strides brought him to Daniel's side, and his eyes were moist with emotion.

Daniel slapped Germaine in the chest with the back of his hand. "Hop back to Bailemor—now!" His emphatic gaze told Germaine not to argue.

In the distance, they heard voices yelling. Above all was the squeaky, fear-shaken voice of Julian. "Get after them! Don't let them escape!"

Daniel turned to Nolan. "When did you take your last pill?"

"This morning," he replied through hurried breaths.

"Good. It's time for you to hop, but we need a little space between us and the Kaezzarites." Daniel turned toward the deeper, dark woods. "Run!"

All three men accelerated, bounding over fallen logs, while the smaller twigs and ferns whipped against their bodies. Nolan saw the ripples begin to form around Germaine, his body distorted, pulling back into long strips of color as if someone was stretching him. Then, he was gone.

Daniel and Nolan ran even faster, headlong through the dark trees. The ominous, thick cloud-cover created a landscape devoid of light for the men to attempt their escape through. They each fell several times, but as they were helped up by the other, they were compelled to run even faster. They were hastened by the livid voices of their pursuers and the explosions of orange light behind them. The pursuers threw burst after burst ahead of them, searching for their Celtae prey in the forest darkness. One such burst exploded against a large rock close to Daniel, and sparks of orange light careened in all directions. In the light, both men saw a log lying across their path, and the distance was imprinted in their minds as the light faded. They both leapt at the same moment just as another burst exploded off the tree to Nolan's left. The bright light lit up the chasm, but it was too late. They were both airborne while the ground was left behind, their arms and legs flailed over the 200-foot precipice.

Nolan closed his eyes. His new found instincts quickly pushed the Athar into his mind. The markers lit up like matches striking on sandpaper, but he didn't know which one to choose or where to focus?

At that moment, he felt Daniel's strong fingers grasp his shoulder as they both plummeted toward the sharp rocks far below. The Athar burst to ever brighter hues as if filters had been removed. One marker flashed brilliantly. *That was it!* He focused on the marker, causing an almost instantaneous feeling of butterflies in his stomach and a sense of vertigo. He wondered if this was due to his fear, or was he on his way?

Julian's short legs held back the Kaezzarite's pursuit. The others were faster, but they dared not leave their leader behind. Their bursts showed them the deep chasm, giving them plenty of time to stop at the edge. Julian peered down, firing a burst into the depths. It crashed against the rocks below. The thin river running through the winding valley was lit up with a shower of sparks. There was no sign of either man—nothing. Julian threw another burst. It landed in the water with a sizzle, and the refracted light illuminated the water for a hundred feet in each direction. Again, there was no sign of either man. Julian knew they were gone from this forest and from this Earth, but he continued to unleash burst after burst into the depths of the chasm. His comrades slowly backed off, seeing his face contorted with rage, his frothing lips repeating over and over, "No. No… NO… NO… NOOOO!!"

Nolan and Daniel had vanished.

The story continues in Wyld Wynd The Unrest, book two of the Wyld Wynd Series.

Dear Reader:

Reviews are important to every author. We are thankful that many readers take a few moments to return to the purchasing website, in this case, Amazon, and leave a rating and a review.

If you could do so for this story, it would be much appreciated. Keep in mind, a Hollywood style review is not needed. Even a few simple words would be great.

Thanks again, and I hope you enjoyed the story.

Peter Sandor

www.ingramcontent.com/pod-product-compliance
Lightning Source LLC
Chambersburg PA
CBHW031125210626
46816CB00016B/2375